EMMA TENNANT

The Harp Lesson

OTHER FICTION

EMMA TENNANT

The Harp Lesson

MAIA

Published in 2005 by
The Maia Press Limited
82 Forest Road
London E8 3BH
www.maiapress.com

ISBN 1 904559 16 6

A CIP catalogue record for this book is available
from the British Library

Printed and bound in Great Britain by Thanet Press

The publisher gratefully acknowledges support
from Arts Council England

Foreword

My grandmother Pamela was born in 1871 into an English family in Wiltshire which liked to see itself as both French and Irish. She told my father the story of her early years in the house west of Salisbury where she grew up, surrounded by the works of those most English of artists and thinkers, William Morris, E. Burne-Jones and Philip Webb – and how, despite this renaissance in design and political attitudes in England, the tales of her French grandmother and their interest to the whole family made the hearing of them stand out as the most exciting and significant times in her memory.

My grandmother's grandmother, Pamela Campbell, had been known as a child as Little Pam. She was born in Dublin at the time of the Irish Rebellion instigated by her father, Lord Edward Fitzgerald. My grandmother told her children that the life of Little Pam's mother, La Belle Pamela, had been both extraordinary and romantic. It was little wonder her descendants clung to this connection, inheriting their Frenchness and Irishness from La Belle Pamela and the dashing revolutionary she married, Lord Edward.

My grandmother never knew Little Pam. She died two years before my grandmother was born, but the link she provided with the past fascinated this last of the Pamelas – most of all the stories about Little Pam's mother, La Belle Pamela. An orphan adopted into the family of Madame de Genlis in the 1780s, Pamela had been assumed by contemporaries to be the natural child of Madame de Genlis and Philippe Égalité, Duc de Chartres and later Duc d'Orléans.

My grandmother loved to hear the story of how her own grandmother Pam Campbell had wished to pass on to the granddaughter she said should be called after the famous Pamela the account of her childhood in Paris after Little Pam's father, Lord Edward Fitzgerald, had died in Dublin Castle in the Irish insurrection. When La Belle Pamela, no longer able to support her daughter, had sent her away from Paris to London, Little Pam remembered her sadness at having to leave her mother. A barrel organ was playing in the street as she left and she had never been able since to hear the sound without feeling that sadness.

The children liked most of all to hear about the French Revolution, and La Belle Pamela's life in the Palais Royal in Paris, right in the thick of the fighting and plotting that brought down the French monarchy.

They liked, too, to hear of Pamela's life in Ireland, and of the French soldiers who tried to land their ships in Bantry Bay, to aid the Irish rebels headed by the revolutionary Lord Edward. That these two fascinating characters were the parents of their stout, kindly grandmother made her doubly glamorous in their eyes. Even though she had never known her, my grandmother Pamela had understood the excitement and strangeness which had accompanied a visit from Little Pam. All the time Little Pam was there, in this most English of country houses, people felt themselves transported to France. When she died, my grandmother's elder brothers and sisters thought they heard a barrel organ play under the bedroom windows, in the house on the Wiltshire downs.

Little Pam wrote down her mother's memories before she died, and she dedicated them to the granddaughter who was to be the next Pamela. When Pamela married and her children were old enough to understand, they in turn fell under the spell of La Belle Pamela, so her story was passed down the family, in this way, more told aloud than read.

Here it is.

Chapter 1

V

Pamela

I am in a field, it is spring and there are long grasses where yellow butterflies fly in and out. It is sunny, but the earth is damp under the blanket I've been left to lie on until someone remembers to come and lift me up.

I know I'm waiting for her, the woman who laughs with her friends along the river bank. She's in a loose-fitting dress that is the same colour as the butterflies. She comes towards me and as she leans over she opens and closes her mouth, saying the word over and over again. Her teeth are strong and white, and I can smell the hair that coils down as far as her breasts. But I won't be fed by the laughing woman in the yellow dress. I know, already, that she is not to be trusted. And I sense, somehow, that the friends who leave the river bank to join her, in their loose hair and simple dresses, are play-acting, just like the woman who mouths down at me without a sound. 'Maman,' the teeth say, 'Maman.'

Y

I can no more say this memory is true than insist it never happened. I do know that all my life I have received strange looks and questions: am I by birth English or French, was my mother, the famous and learned royal tutor who denied so often that I was her child, in fact lying or telling the truth? The day in the long grass seems real, to me: but did I take on the infancy of another and make it my dream? It is impossible to tell. And this woman – whom I see running towards me from the river bank – why should so many consider her to be my mother, if she was not?

The Comtesse de Genlis is her name. By the time I tell this to you, she will be dead and I shall follow her shortly to the grave. It is fifty years since I was brought to Paris and placed first in the arms of the man they say was my father, Philippe Duc de Chartres, and then handed with tenderness to Madame de Genlis. And my memory – of the woman who ran across the meadows by the river in France and who stared down at me on my fleece in a fit of maternal affection – is succeeded by others as treacherous as the first. Wherever there was power, influence and wealth, the Comtesse would make sure she was included. From the day she entered the royal household of the Duc d'Orléans and his son Philippe, she would plot and plan her own advancement. She has known life in the Revolution, has befriended Napoleon and now, in her last moments, she sees Philippe's son, her old pupil, ascend to the throne of France.

Yet, for all her wickedness and cunning, I loved my mother, who wrote romances that showed her passion for the daughter she had had with Philippe. I loved her wit, and I prayed for her approval. The mother I had left behind in England I soon forgot; though some said she actually was the one who gave birth to me, in a place covered with snow and ice, where it was black as night all winter long.

Y

Mary Sims was her name, and my life with her is easy to remember, perhaps because the sheer monotony of the days formed a pattern in my mind that all the succeeding years failed to obliterate.

We lived in Dorset, on the southern coast of England, in a small town called Christchurch. My name was Nancy, then; and Mrs Sims my mother would take me sometimes to the great lagoon formed by the sea at Chesil Beach. There were high banks of gravel there, and swans as dingy-looking as the laundry Mary took in to make a living. I had no idea at the time that this woman with her fine, tired features and hands that had a hundred tiny inlets in the skin – like the streams that run to meet high tide at our famous beach – was known as a Bristol-woman – that is, a woman of easy virtue. It couldn't occur to me that the sheets she rolled and thumped, the quilts that hung damp in the sea air out the back of our tiny Christchurch house and the long gentlemen's shirts that had seen better days, could not supply my mother's needs. Perhaps, as I thought later when I looked back at the ease with which she let me go, this was the reason: Mary Sims had no one to support her, and the money the tall man in the velvet jacket brought her was a necessity. But by the time I was old enough to realise this I knew the tall man had been sent by the one they call my father, the cousin of the King of France, Philippe Duc de Chartres.

γ

'Seals – and fishing,' Mary Sims said, as we sat one day on the high gravel bank overlooking the sea. The lagoon lay behind us, and the swans, which were nesting and so could not be disturbed, sat on their bundles of twigs and grass on the north side, by pens where their young would be placed when they were of the right age. I must have known even then, I suppose – this was after the first visit of the man in the velvet coat – that I, like the cobs in their fluffy brown feathers, would be taken from the woman I knew as my mother, and that I might never see her again. 'I'll tell you about the island,' Mary Sims said. 'Can you remember the name of the place where you were born?'

Instead of answering, I hugged my knees together and shifted on the hard pebbles before going on with my endless staring out to sea. One of the women who came and helped out on washdays, Dora, had said she'd met a French sailor, rescued from some wreck on the Dorset coast, and he'd promised to take her across to his country, rowing in a little boat he'd found in a cove up beyond West Bay. 'You'd be lucky,' my mother had retorted, and the great pans steamed and hissed as she pushed through the sheets and pillow-cases of the Christchurch gentry (for some reason, Mary Sims boasted that she only did the washing for the better sort of people; some days she even said she belonged to a good family herself, and our name was really Seymour). 'You'd soon lose everything you've got, if you go to that place France,' Mary said.

Now, as I bring the scene to my mind, I realise that I was that day in a sulky mood. As I say, I had a suspicion that change was under way; and, maybe because I'd been through changes earlier (after all, I was only six years old at the time and the persistently strong picture of the woman by the river bank showed I'd undergone some upheaval or another when very small), I didn't want to hear what Mary was going to tell me. I knew the name of the place which she'd told me over and over again was the island very far north where she'd lived with the seal-hunter William Brixey; I knew the stories of seal pie and the jet-black nights that never gave way to the sun at all. 'He'll come back and we'll be with him again,' Mary, my mother, said. 'They always go out in early spring and he'll be back by summer. If you think hard, Nancy, you'll see the place and then you'll recognise your father when he comes. Mr Brixey – ' and then she fell silent, as she always did; for of course the great seal hunter William Brixey never came.

Then, as a sharp easterly wind blew down the coast, and we both rose from the gravel bank to slither down to the shelter of the Swannery and the green fields around St Catherine's Church, Mary Sims delivered the blow I had suspected was coming all along. 'I've something to tell you, child,' she said; and I felt a sudden tugging at my heart as if I'd climbed too fast to the top of the hill that looks down on the village of Abbotsbury. I was far from home. I wanted to run back there, with Mary, pale and strained in the April sunlight, trying to catch me as I ran. I needed the comfort of the piles of soiled linen left by the good people of Christchurch, in the outhouse we left unlocked by the side of the house; and the routine of carrying it in, ready for the wash. Everything, as I willed it, must go on being just the same.

'The gentleman came again today while you were still sleeping,' Mary Sims said. 'He's taking you to Paris – ' and, on seeing the blankness on my face as I stopped, standing quite still on the hillside high above the place where the birds cared for by the swanherd are made ready for their entrance to the lagoon, '– France.'

γ

Mr Forth is not like the other gentlemen who come, saying they've left a fob watch in their shirt pocket or

that a fine ring slipped down in the bed and got lost in
the sheets – all lies, as I found out, for what they want is
to be alone with Mary Sims. If William Brixey does
come back, with the smell of cod and herring on him
(that is all I remember of the man Mary says is my
father), then the fine gentlemen will be told not to come.
For a moment, when we rounded the corner of the lane
with the row of cottages that makes up the main street
of Christchurch, I believed the man with his back to us
by the front door might be the man my mother has seen
most of, lately: the bailiff to the estates of the Fox
family, who own all the land around here. I've been
taught to curtsey when that man arrives, in his velvet
coat and a shabby hat that shows him to be a real
country gentleman. Mary has to pay rent to Mr Fox's
man, and I've seen him press the coins back in her hand
as he leaves. But today, as I can't help realising, a very
different transaction is about to take place. The man
who turns to see us I have not seen here before. He has
a mass of powdered hair and his velvet coat has four
gold buttons. His cravat comes right up over his chin
and his face is like a sheep's face, the white cravat
beneath like a plate with this solemn face served on it.
Monsieur Mouton, I call the gentleman Mary intro-
duces as Mr Nathaniel Forth. A sheep who will do as he
is told by the most important master, as I was to learn.

'This was my instruction,' the elegantly attired Mr
Forth informs my mother. 'To bring back a fine mare
and a pretty little girl with dark hair, to be playmate for

the three-year-old twin daughters of the Duc de Chartres. She must not speak a word of French – ' and here Mr Mouton bends down and tweaks my ear, a gesture I have always hated in the visitors to Mary's laundry, 'You can assure me of that, I expect, Mrs Sims?'

'Not a word,' Mary says. I hate her at that moment, for she looks admiringly up at the sheep's-head-on-a-plate, and I glance by force of habit at the purse she wears on a string on her waist – which, as it happens, both Mr Forth and Mary are gazing at intently as they converse.

'And our pretty little girl must not have a long nose,' the sheep goes on. 'The Duc was particularly keen that this rule should be observed.'

'Well, you can see she has not,' replies Mary. A vague look comes into her eyes, as a horse coming up the lane can distinctly be heard. This could be Mr Fox's bailiff – and even I know that Mary has no desire to be found standing just inside the porch of her tiny house with a scented and powdered man of a far more elevated rank than the bailiff. 'I am charged by the royal house of Bourbon,' Mr Forth says in one long, swooping rush of words, 'to offer you this emolument, dear Mrs Sims, for your pains. Little Anne here – '

'We call her Nancy,' Mary says. As someone dismounts from the horse outside, she draws us all into the front room, where – try as she may to keep it away from some part of our home – the washing lies in bundles by the fireplace and on each chair and stool. I see her reach out for the gold; Mr Forth, aware as we are of a loud knocking on our door, is as quick to hand it over.

'We'll leave this way,' my mother says, and she picks up a bag I now see must have been packed ready before we went walking above Chesil Beach today. I feel the fear, the quickening in my stomach, the sudden attack of nausea which comes to me when – as alas so frequently has been the case – I am threatened with a great change in my way of life.

'We sail tonight,' Mr Sheep declares, when Mary has slid the coins into her purse. She stoops to kiss me, my humble cotton bag already in her hand, and I feel another tweak from the odious Mr Forth. 'Our Nancy will not be sea-sick, I trust. We had to wait, with these spring tides, a full three days before we could embark at Calais.'

This was when I knew that Mary Sims betrayed me. For – just as I kept (and sometimes treasured) that memory of the fine lady on the river bank and the word she murmured to me with a love the washerwoman never showed – I also knew I had no memory whatso-ever of being in a vessel on the sea.

'Oh, Nancy will not suffer in the slightest,' Mary assured Mr Nathaniel Forth. 'After all, she was brought over from France as an infant, as you must know.'

Mr Forth bowed in acquiescence – although I could see he was new to this arrangement and had as little knowledge of my past as I did. With a word of regret at having to banish her visitor so speedily, Mrs Sims then ushered him from the back door, where I could see a horse was tethered, munching at the thin grass in our strip of garden.

'You see, I succeeded in finding a very fine mare for the Duc de Chartres,' Mr Forth cried, his white hair pulling out from his head in the strong wind. 'And a pretty child, just as requested. Madam, this has been a fortunate day.'

But my mother had turned on her heel and I heard the back door lock behind her as she went to greet her new visitor in the lane.

I was first lifted up, then seated in front of the man who had just bought me, the emissary of the Duc de Chartres. We rode until we arrived at the port of Dover. The sea was too rough to set sail that night, and the next day we left for France.

And that was the last I saw of Mary Sims, also known as Mrs William Brixey.

Chapter 2

Y

Pamela

The sea was rough on this Channel which my mother told me I had been brought over when I was still too young to understand where or who I might be. Mr Forth sat below in his cabin; and after a while he made no effort to stop me running up on deck. I stood, my hands grabbing the rail and my feet skidding under me as the waves washed into the boat. I saw the white cliffs, as Mr Forth had told me they were. 'Has no one told you anything of the country where I found you?' he said, and he laughed, the sheep, so that his wig bounced and the gold buttons on his coat twinkled in the sunlight. 'A foundling indeed,' he went on, 'and without the good Reverend Jeans one who might have been lost to Madame La Comtesse forever.'

I was too impatient to run aloft, to wonder what this man meant, who first had told my mother Mary Sims that a Monsieur Le Duc wished for him to bring a child to France, and now spoke to me of a Madame La Comtesse. I had seen a countess, for there was one such in Dorset, where we lived; and we saw her down by the Swannery from time to time, walking round a walled garden with a man who carried tall, spiky trees in pots. The Countess was forming an exotic garden, so Mary told me; and these were palms. So as soon as Mr Forth spoke of a Comtesse, I imagined her with creepers falling down over her head from the huge trees she lived amongst. I didn't like the idea, and began to cry.

'Madame has brought you this,' Mr Forth said, when I was halfway up the steps to the deck again. For the strange part is that I was homesick, a feeling I had never known before. Mary, who had been so often indifferent or bad-tempered and who had irritated me with the memories she tried to make me have, of Fogo Island in Newfoundland and William Brixey, my father who hunted seals for their skins, was fast becoming precious to me. And, like any emigrant, I wanted to stay on deck and see the cliffs, white and receding in a spray of mist and spring rain. I think I knew that I might never return to Christchurch, or the huge copper pans where the washing bubbled and steamed all day long.

'Wait, Nancy,' Mister Forth said, and he opened his bag and pulled out something wrapped in a dark cloth. I stood suspicious a while and he took advantage of my hesitation: in all probability he had no notion of the fact I had never received anything for myself in all my life, that my dresses and shoes were hand-me-downs procured by Mary Sims in return for a load of laundry, and that the only time I saw anything brought out of a bag was the occasion of Mary's brother, a poacher, coming into our little cottage and looking over his shoulder before pulling a brace of partridges or a hare from his sack.

Mr Forth's bag was as elegant as his tailored coat and breeches. And, as I soon saw, it was also a coat which came from the wrapping of black cloth, when he had taken it from the bag. He unwrapped it, smiling and talking as he did so, but I cannot say I listened to a word, for the coat – as he had perhaps known all along – was so dazzling to me that I could think of nothing else. The ruby velvet – for this it was – shone in the darkness of the cabin, where a narrow porthole allowed no more than a glimpse occasionally of the sun. The cabin was otherwise lit only by a lamp. He held it out to me, this coat so utterly unlike anything I had worn or even seen – for at the estate parties at the Countess's great mansion at Abbotsbury the children of the nobility had never appeared in a garment of such beauty – and I saw myself stretch out my arms to take it, like a gift in a dream. 'Put it on!' ordered Mr Forth, and I was grateful to him that he didn't fuss me with the way to find the armholes and the rest of it, as Mary my mother would have done.

'Red Riding Hood,' said Mr Forth, and for a moment I was afraid of this sheep who suddenly looked across at me in the gloom of the cabin like a wolf. 'Madame will be pleased, she has taken enough trouble over this,' Forth continued, but more as if he was speaking to himself. 'And the Duc de Chartres will be delighted with this new companion for his daughters.'

I stayed only a second longer before running up on deck at last. The salt spray hit my face like a whip and my hair was drenched immediately, so I pulled up the hood of the little cloak and hugged the velvet closer to my body.

When I looked out at the sea and the white cliffs of Dover, the white cliffs had gone.

$\mathcal{Y}$

I don't know how many hours it took to arrive in Paris. But after we had entered the grand carriage – which seemed to be waiting for Mr Forth like the coach in the Cinderella story Mary Sims used to tell me when I was half asleep by the fire and the washing was already done – we moved through a landscape that was green and light, with a pretty blue sky hanging over it, this dappled with white clouds. I must have slept then, thinking myself a part of the fairy story Mary knew by heart: the coach, the princess whose beautiful dress turns back to rags at midnight, the postilions who go back to being frogs or toads. I looked out of the window and saw that it was now dark. And, through all this, the fine mare Mr Forth had bought in England for the man I imagined to be his master galloped along behind us. The fields on either side of the thin road were a different shape from those in England – I think I saw that, but really I remember the horse, and Mr Forth sleeping with his wig askew, against the silk cushions.

So it was late when we finally arrived at the great palace. Even as Mr Forth lifted me out of the carriage, I saw the house we had come to was ten times bigger than the mansion where the Earl and Countess live on the Dorset estate which I thought then had no boundaries. It was huge, the palace, and I also saw – as the 'ambassador' (for this was the name Mr Forth said I should use when I spoke of him to my new hosts) held me high as if showing off a trophy to an invisible audience – that this magnificent building did indeed have boundaries, and that these enclosed a magical city.

'Well, little one,' the Sheep muttered in my ear, so that I had to pull away from his sickly breath, a smell that was dark and rusty and sweet at the same time. 'What do you say to living here, are you not a fortunate child?'

Before I could show I had no wish to answer, I found myself set down at a side door to the palace; and, on the way, still in my high place on the shoulders of the odious Mr Forth, I could see that some of this city within the walls was unfinished, and under construction. There were booths with lanterns, and what appeared to be mechanical people, as tall as humans but stiff and strange-looking, dancing in open-sided halls with roofs that appeared to be made from palm-leaves like those in the exotic garden where the English Countess tends her plants. There was wooden scaffolding, and the shapes of new, unimaginable buildings, shrouded within; and a walkway, also wooden but solid and well-built, where ladies leaned down to look at us, and a crowd was called to witness my arrival.

'Every possible piece of riffraff in the world,' Mr Forth said in a cross tone I hadn't heard before, as he went faster to the side door. 'Now curtsey if you know how,' Mr Forth said with a sneer.

The man who stood by the side entrance to what I was later to be informed was the Palais d'Orléans stepped forward as I was lowered to the ground. He had a full face, black curls and his nose was long. His lips curved and were half-breaking into a smile. He greeted Mr Forth – at least I suppose he must have done, for I have no memory of anything other than the odd effect his face had on me. It was as if, I later felt, this stranger showed each feeling on his features, and it would be a cruel thing to find his great black eyes burn with hatred in one's direction. His mouth showed a love of laughter, but he also liked to inflict pain.

The Duc de Chartres – for so, with great pomposity, Mr Forth introduced him – in turn lifted me up and we went indoors, the door shutting out Forth entirely. I could still hear the words of the self-styled ambassador as I was carried down a maze of passages, all narrow and dimly lit. Mr Forth would like Monsieur Le Duc to know that a fine mare had been found for him, at Newmarket, and would be ready for inspection tomorrow. Mr Forth hopes to present his compliments to the Duc and Duchesse and also to the Gouvernante of their esteemed children, Madame La Comtesse de Genlis – and so on.

But the voice of the Ambassador faded soon, and I found myself carried into a small room, very ornately furnished with mirrors in gold frames and seats upholstered in the finest satins and silks. An oval window at the far end of the room showed the moon looking in through the branches of a tree; and it was just possible to glimpse dancing figures on a stage beyond.

A woman was sitting near the door, on an elegant chair. She looked up as we entered – but it was clear from the expression on her face that this was not the first time she had glanced towards the door and back again.

The man who carried me paused a moment before handing me to her. 'Voilà notre petit bijou,' he said. And, as I was swung between them and finally reached the floor, I heard a sound I could not at first recognise or understand.

They were crying, the man and the woman, softly at first and then louder, as if their outburst of happiness would never end. And when the woman mopped her face and gazed down at me, I knew I disappointed her by pulling away out of reach of her embrace. Yet I knew also that I had seen – and I can only imagine this was the reason for my later fear and mistrust of Félicité de Genlis who had taken such pains to send for me – those chestnut eyes in my earlier life.

In the field, near the river bank: I had seen her there.

Little Pam

My mother was never to know her true parentage. But she soon discovered that she was considered to be the daughter of this brown, thin woman, who treated her sometimes with all the love of a mother long denied the company of her child, and at other times with an indifference and air of disdain that were disconcerting in the extreme.

'I was adopted, so I was told – ' and here my mother would gaze at me entreatingly, as if I, her eldest daughter, could help solve the problem (but I had, in her eyes, become her mother by then, for Pamela, old and ill and dying in a cheap hotel in the Rue Danube, needed me as once I had had need of her). 'I was assumed to be the natural daughter of Félicité de Genlis and Philippe d'Orléans, the man whom they called, in the Revolution, Philippe Egalité. The Duc d'Orléans made over an allowance to me. They both showed me affection, even devotion. But just when the world expected the announcement from Madame de Genlis that I was

indeed their child, the opposite was said. I was Anne or Nancy, daughter of Mary Sims.'

I had as little desire to discuss the cause of my mother's sadness as she had, and we changed the subject, returning to our reminiscences of Ireland, where we had been happy together in the orange and green and white garden by the sea, and going back, in Pamela's case, to her own first days in Paris, when the man she described as having the face of a sheep had brought her to the Palais Royal. She had run in, she said, on the day after her arrival, to a long room packed with people, who had smiled at the child in the red cloak and hood as she made straight for the celebrated governess and mistress of Philippe, the Comtesse de Genlis. 'How was I to know that we were not supposed to have met before?' Pamela said, and she laughed at the memory, reaching for the box of sweet cakes she kept by the side of the bed, as she did so. 'My recognising the woman who taught all the children in her care to call her Maman was proof to the smart friends of the Orléans family that I was the daughter of her liaison with the Duc, I suppose. From then on, with the exception of one or two great ladies who claimed to know better, I was simply Pamela, child of Orléans and Madame de Genlis. But it didn't prevent me, you know, from dreaming of England – or from pining for the life, dull though it may have seemed in comparison, that I had known at Christchurch, near Bournemouth.'

It was true that the Palais d'Orléans, as the magnificent building was originally known, must have come as a shock to a child such as my mother was at the age of six, in 1780. Many of the constructions dreamed up by Philippe, showman and spendthrift, architect of fantasy landscapes and rustic hamlets, were still in the process of being built, it was true: but the atmosphere provided by the palace and its grounds must have been alarming to the small girl brought in from an English fishing village. In fact, the walkways in the gardens of the palace where prostitutes openly flaunted their wares, the coffee houses where the first newspapers were read aloud and seditious ballads were sung, the booths where freaks such as the German giant *Butterbrod* were exhibited, were as new to Parisians as they were to Pamela, though she wasn't to know it. Here, in the heart of a city previously orderly and under control, came the mob, the outsiders, actors, brigands and thieves. And here, as Pamela was the first to discover, were planted the seeds of Revolution that were to surround her all her life.

Madame de Genlis was known as the cleverest and most scheming woman in France. Her husband, kept at a distance in his chateau and vineyard at Sillery and in a house in Paris seldom visited by his wife, appeared happy enough to pursue his own interests without the aid or interference of his wife Félicité DuCrest Saint-Aubin. He gave her up, you might say, while retaining the friendship and patronage of the powerful First Prince of the Blood, Philippe Duc de Chartres – later Orléans – to a life of politics and intrigue, at the Palais Royal.

By the time the 'little foundling Pamela' had appeared there, her 'maman' Madame de Genlis had been appointed governess to the twin daughters of the Duc and Duchesse de Chartres. Shortly after, to underline her importance at the Orléans court, Félicité would receive the title of Governor, responsible for the education of the young princes as well. In order to stress further the purity of her aims and the integrity of her character, the ambitious and pretty tutor demanded a school of her own, where the children could be raised far from the temptations and corruption of Paris. The establishment, at Belle-Chasse, was not far from the town, in fact – Philippe could come and go with ease under the guise of supervising the education of his offspring – but the move was a good one. Félicité, writer of romances and fairy-tales, of philosophical treatises and plays, was astute enough to know that irreproachable behaviour brings higher rewards than the blatant gratification of desires. The little school at the convent at Belle-Chasse was run on the simplest, most frugal and Godfearing principles. My mother's role there, as a sweet young companion for the Chartres children, was to aid them in learning to speak English. For everything English, in those days, was the height of fashion.

As for Philippe – future leader of the camp opposed to his cousins the royal family of France, the man they called my father, whose conduct in the Revolution turned all against him – what kind of man was he? He loved many women, Félicité and my poor mother Pamela amongst them, I have no doubt. His one-time mistress, the beautiful Scotchwoman Grace Elliott, said of him that he was led astray by wicked men, such as Talleyrand and Choderlos de Laclos, whose cynical novel *Les Liaisons Dangereuses* was thought to have been written by Madame de Genlis, so great was the scandal – despite her efforts to safeguard her reputation – which surrounded her. But to judge the self-indulgent, pleasure-loving Philippe by his behaviour with women would lead one to imagine that betrayal came only too easily to him. We can only glimpse the man who stood behind the people – and then lost his head for his pains – through the few words that those who loved him left behind. Pamela, who remained devoted to the man she was taught to see as her Papa, never faltered in her loyalty to him.

Pamela

I am in the schoolroom, a room with bare boards, and windows where the shutters throw shadowy lines on whitewashed walls, lines that dance before my eyes and throw back at me the precepts of Jean-Jacques Rousseau and the simple arithmetic deemed necessary for young princesses of the blood.

I can neither read nor write in this new language I seem to be expected by everyone here to know instinctively. I am dumb, a creature brought forward from my little worktable at the back of the room and demanded to mime 'Héloïse' or 'Virginie' for the interest and delectation of visitors. I must appear passionate, tragic or radiant, at the crack of the tutor's whip. 'Ah, Pamela!' says Madame in a low, amused and yet confiding voice when my audience want to know just who I may be. 'Now, Pamela's story is an interesting one. But this I shall have to tell you later.' And with a smile as full of intrigue and sly compassion as she can make it, 'Maman' sweeps out of our little classroom and we are left with the lines the shutters make on the walls of the old convent, and the coughing of the children brought into this cold, damp building to be taught the 'new ideas' of which our famous tutor speaks.

For all its appearance of great age, the place we occupy is new, recently put up for our esteemed 'Gouverneur'. Madame de Genlis had specified that a pavilion be erected, this joined to the old convent at Belle-Chasse by a long trellised passage; here, the sons and daughters of Monseigneur and selected pupils from high-born families are to be prepared for their future posts and duties. One is to be educated to ascend the throne of France, I hear Henriette say with a giggle she will receive a slap for, if her aunt Félicité catches her whispering what every chambermaid and stable boy at home in the great house by the river in Paris knows very well already. For it is no secret that 'Maman' is teaching the Orléans children to look forward to royal status. They have the right, by blood, to all the great estates and palaces at present enjoyed by our King and his Austrian Queen: Versailles, where Papa – as I may call him when we are alone together – will take me to see fountains as tall as a man, dancing in the sunlight like the diamond cockade my father pins in his hat; Marly, where the flowers are made of brightly painted wood and are stuck each morning in the ground; and Fontainebleau, with a forest so thick around the castle that the King of France may hunt boar each day of his life. If his plans succeed, all these will belong to the Duc

de Chartres, when once he has succeeded to the
Bourbon throne, and his son, Louis-Philippe, will follow
him. But, for the moment, as Henriette clamps her hand
over her mouth in an attempt to quell her giggling
(a distinguished visitor had just come and gone, and
has favourably compared the educational practices
of Madame de Genlis with those of the tutors to the
Royal Family: 'Ah yes,' replied Maman, our proud
Gouverneur, 'We take our princes and princesses out
into the world. They are not confined, as the royal children are, with Greek and Latin and German, in their
palaces'), there is no time to relate further the glories
and riches which will come to the children of Orléans.
The distinguished visitor, impressed, bowing, has left
the classroom, without so much as a glimpse of the
naughty expression on the face of Henriette.

My life here would be unbearable, if it were not for
Henriette. If I am truly the daughter of Madame de
Genlis, then Henriette de Sercey is my first cousin: if I
am not, but originate, as I do from time to time believe,
in Dorset and Newfoundland, child of the cod and salt
trade, owing my name and life to a man named William
Brixey and his common-law wife Mary Sims, then this
will only go to prove that friendship, such as I have
for my dear Henriette, does not depend on kinship or
even on a shared past. We are all born equal and also
unalike. Madame teaches this 'equality' and Papa,
whom the crowds love when he rides or walks out from
his Palais d'Orléans, proclaims it also. Yet I notice that

none of those who speak or write of it do so for long, before returning to speak of their cousinships and inheritances, their great titles and estates.

Now Maman calls us to come out in the open air. We file out, into the neat gardens of the convent at Belle-Chasse. Here we are, in a painting I have kept from those days: a miniature, rather, which shows our little lives playing out in a world without change or menace, a world described by Maman's good friend and confidant M. Talleyrand, as belonging to an age of ease, of which later generations would be ignorant. We chase the ball, against a fairy-tale moonscape; we run forever in the oval frame, in those soft, innocent days. 'Poor' Henriette (she received this appellation from Maman, who saw her niece was not pretty; was plump as a pudding, in fact, and with a face that is fat and round, but the artist disguises this) runs too; and the surviving twin of the Duchesse de Chartres, known as Mademoiselle. We run, endlessly pursuing the golden ball – of marriage, of motherhood, of happiness. We do not belong in a real world, at all.

Little Pam

My mother had often tried to describe to me the *douceur de vivre* as defined by M. Talleyrand, of those days before the Revolution. The old Duc de —— , for instance, would lie in bed in his house in the Faubourg St Honoré while a couple of cows, imported into the household and accommodated in mangers in a simulacrum of a byre, munched their hay just a few feet from his side. Madame de Genlis, the tireless plotter for the Orléans cause – and for her own ambition also, it goes without saying – had taken her Pamela there, and the old man had commented on the beauty of the child, and on her different-coloured eyes. In this, he said, he was reminded of a young lady of the Court of King Louis and Marie-Antoinette who, lovely as the mysterious Pamela, had fallen in love with a handsome young Count dead at the age of twenty-one and therefore destined never to be her husband. The Count's double, an illegitimate half-brother, had appeared at Court one day, so the old Duc related; and the young beauty had fainted away in front of the Queen. My mother remembered the telling of this story for she, too, was to enter a world of doubles: it seemed sometimes, she said in a burst of animation towards the end of her life, that she was two people, and had attracted two men, both of whom had been passionately enamoured of her other being. Then she would fall back on her pillows and ask me to bring her water and a plate of the profiteroles she loved to eat, the pastry as soft and crumbling as her memories of those long-gone days.

If Pamela was indulged, like the princes Monpensier, Beaujolais and the heir Louis-Philippe, sons of Philippe Duc de Chartres – along with Mademoiselle, his daughter – then Madame de Genlis never allowed them to forget the existence of the mob, of those who were later to call 'Vive Orléans' and 'Vive Necker' (the Finance Minister) and hold up busts of their heroes in the street. There might be amusements and imaginary kingdoms – did not the Marquis de Sillery, as Madame's husband now was, construct seven islands in the river on his estate, the largest named Félicité, 'happiness', after his clever and disloyal wife? – but the children were reminded at every turn of what makes up a true kingdom and fuels its power: the mob. With an eye to the people, 'Maman' is seen to lead her charges to the Mont St Michel, where young Louis-Philippe demolishes a wooden cage, relic of a slaveship, with his small axe. Madame speaks of the poor when she is out in the world, and she sends Pamela, dressed as a grey sister, a nun of an order that ministers to the unfortunate, the derelict, the starving, with food and alms, to the worst districts within a few leagues of Paris or Belle-Chasse. And while she does this, support for her lover Philippe d'Orléans grows; and King Louis goes hunting in the forest at Fontainbleau and the Queen, Marie-Antoinette, plays at dairymaid at the Trianon. She too has cows tended by footmen, waited on like royalty. The people will turn – and they will turn to Philippe and place him on the throne. Madame dreams of the divorce and disappearance of Philippe's wife, the Duchesse de Chartres, and of her own role in the new state. If Philippe will listen to advice; if he will leave his mistresses to give time to the woman who educates his children and rules his head if not always his heart, France will fall into their hands.

Of course, my mother couldn't know any of this. She knew only that she loved the man, said to be her father, who in turn loved amusements and pleasure, the construction of the joke, the idle fancy, the designing of a mock community, more than any other thing. Was Pamela, one eye light grey as the English Channel, the other stormy dark, no more than another passing interest, to be discarded when she married or grew old? Was this daughter, with her carefully declared antecedents, an English item for a collector, like a whip or a riding-coat? It seems not, and that an affection lasted between the man who came to be seen as the

greatest traitor of the age and the child known as La
Belle Pamela. Her beauty would not endure; nor would
the popularity of Philippe Egalité, the name chosen by
Orléans in the third year of the Revolution. He would
die like the rest, on the guillotine; and so great was
Pamela's love for him that news of his death was for
months withheld from her in her new home across the
sea.

They were, perhaps, Philippe and the adopted
daughter reared in the seedbed of the Revolution, both
acting out parts for which they had neither preparation
nor real inclination. My mother would have preferred, I
dare say, to have returned to 'normality' as she did as a
child when the portable theatre introduced by 'Maman'
was, along with the dressing-up box, put away.
Philippe, led further and further into revolutionary
activities by the friends and accomplices of Madame de
Genlis, found it was too late, once the mob was truly
aroused, to return to his hobby of erecting model
villages, each equipped with windmills and streams of
clear running water.

So – if I'm asked, as I so often am – if I believe
Pamela to have been in truth the daughter of Philippe
d'Orléans, I reply that there are indeed similarities
between them. Philippe was the great pretender – of
faith in the chimera, equality, and of a liberty he knew
came with the privilege he had all his life enjoyed.
Pamela Sims, as she was formally known at the Court of
Orléans, was brought up to dissemble: she was and was

not the child of Philippe and Félicité. She must live life
as an open secret; and I believe she was very much
wounded by the demands imposed on her. 'Pamela, do
Héloïse!' – even in old age my mother would sketch out
the scene, the 'attitude' of a beautiful young woman,
kneeling and gazing imploringly at a passion that came
from a novel, and not from life.

Pamela

What was he like, this man whom I must address as Monseigneur in public and whom everyone said loved me and was my true father? Was he as frivolous and undependable as his enemies made him out to be – or did he start, in fact, with a revulsion to the ways at the court of his cousin, King Louis, and an instinctive sense of indignation at the poverty of the French people: the famines, the heavy taxes, the heartlessness of this age of *douceur de vivre*? I found him, when I was still a child, much like a child himself, this Prince who wished to proclaim equality and liberty for all; and, as any child would do, I admired his helpless anger in the face of injustice and cynicism and followed him blindly in what appeared to be his totally altruistic opinions and plans of action. It didn't occur to me until much later that a loathing of the Queen, intensified by slights apparently administered by the King himself, lay at the root of the revolutionary aims of the Duc d'Orléans.

It so happened that I was witness, though I didn't fully understand this at the time, of the snub to my father which hardened his heart against the monarchy permanently. This was the refusal on the part of the King to permit a betrothal between the daughter of the Duc and Duchesse de Chartres and the King's nephew, the Vicomte d'Angouleme. From that day, Philippe spoke more and more ill of the royal family – and in particular of Marie-Antoinette – and I honestly believe that the fury whipped up against the Queen (I hold out to you now the miniature my poor dear Henriette had of her idol, with the words *Assassinée helas!* written beneath her image), I do truly believe the Revolution we all welcomed with such fervour at the Palais-Royal would not have taken place if my father had not been instrumental in fanning the flames of hatred against the woman they called the 'Austrian Queen' of France.

He had taken me to Versailles on this occasion, and (it was not for the first time) – Philippe enjoying, I believe, the comments on my beauty made by all who saw me perched on his shoulder, and happy to take me with him on his visits to his mistresses past and present (this naturally unknown to Maman: I was told to keep silent) – he set me down in the gardens of the great Palace, called to a lady-in-waiting to keep an eye on me, and set off for his interview with the King.

This time, however, I must have decided I was bored with the monumental architecture, the fountains and the great basins of water where gold and red fish swam round and round. I had no desire, either, to visit the petit Trianon, which the lady-in-waiting, a pretty girl of about fifteen, offered me in the way of amusement; I had seen the dairy, and the Queen's pet rabbits, and had had pointed out to me the roses and gillyflowers in pots on the windowsills of those cottages which had no real life away from the make-believe of a simple rustic existence. I wanted to follow the man I loved and felt such pride for, the first Prince of the Blood, into the palace itself. And I persuaded the lady-in-waiting, who had little else to do, to conceal me under a wide shawl and take me into the *salle* where the women glided on the parquet floor without once lifting their feet, and Papa, along with a select company of other men of high rank, handed His Majesty his shirt and in general assisted him with his *levée*.

There was no difficulty in prodding my carrier to take me as near to the Royal scene as she was able. I could see my father, his most agreeable expression on his face, take the shirt from a nobleman near the chair where the King sat waiting for the ritual to continue. I saw Philippe bow and hand the shirt to the King. And I saw the King refuse to accept it from the hands of his cousin, and look away in distaste from him. The incident passed in a matter of seconds, and another courtier took charge of the shirt. But the Duc de Chartres, slighted as he had been, walked very sharply from the cluster around the monarch and out over the long parquet floor to the portal leading to the gardens. It was as much as my poor young lady-in-waiting could do, to glide at an unseemly speed after him, pull back the shawl, and announce we had been playing Puss-in-the-Corner at the Trianon, to while away the time. Papa, with a distracted air, accepted this and took me up in his arms to embrace me, before setting me down on the ground and announcing that we must go and find our carriage, there would be no more games at Versailles today. 'Nor, indeed, ever again,' I heard him mutter, as I ran to keep up with him over the fine green grass. And I came to realise he had meant what he said: since that day, Monseigneur the future Duc d'Orléans did not visit the King and Queen at Versailles. I believe he thought the King hated him.

Little Pam

I will never know if my mother understood the changing world in which her sudden adoption by the clever governess Madame de Genlis had plunged her. What she made of the Palais Royal, with its gardens lit at night with lamps, its armies of agitators at Foy's and in the coffee houses where the journalists loved to call out greetings of affectionate mockery to the daughter of the budding Revolution, is impossible to tell. This motley crowd, a fairground show of monsters and sedition, was her home, with Belle-Chasse a counterpart both innocent and sinister – sinister in that 'Maman' in her blue-upholstered salon there would mastermind the plans for overthrowing the King and placing Philippe in a position where he could be declared Regent; and at the same time this perfect Maman preached simplicity and purity to the children of the man she was determined to see on the throne. Pamela, by the age of twelve, was greeted with increasing fervour by the swelling Jacobin faction, and must have been expected to see herself as a future member of a royal house – though I don't believe she was in any way affected by the compliments and assurances from those who joined the Orléanistes in their desire to rid the country of the corruption of Versailles. 'The pity was,' my mother would confide when I was a child still, her other two safely in England and Ireland, cared for by our father's family, the Fitzgeralds, 'that M. d'Orléans lost his popularity when he fled to England at the time the King and Queen were brought into Paris from Versailles. But he was in danger: General Lafayette had decided to protect the royal family, and Philippe was now considered to be the treasurer of the Revolution. What else could he do?'

And Pamela – La Belle Pamela, whose beauty, in my eyes at least, had not faded over all the years of her sufferings at the hands of the woman who never could bring herself to confess she was her true mother – would gaze from the window of her bedroom in the hotel in the Rue Danube and smile. She knew, as she had told me with absolute sincerity on many occasions, that 'Maman' had loved her; and, oddest of all the governess's whimsical and inexplicable decisions, had felt no love for her 'sister,' also considered to be her daughter with Philippe, who arrived at the Palais Royal two years after Pamela was brought there by Monsieur Forth. Hermine, as the child was named, was handed over to the daughter of Madame de Genlis with her legal husband, and brought up away from Madame.

What all this could have meant to my mother I cannot say: she was cheerful sometimes, melancholic at others. But she declared that she was glad Madame de Genlis still lived, to see her pupil, Philippe's son, come at last to the throne. And I knew also, from her accounts of those strange and terrifying times, that the man in whom the governess had placed all her hopes, her lover the Duc d'Orléans, had at a crucial moment rescinded his claim to the Regency and thus had said farewell to his early ambitions to become King of France. At that instant, Madame de Genlis in turn gave up her devotion to Philippe and concentrated instead on his son. It was a triumph very typical of the woman who plotted and planned for power all her life, that she lived just long enough to see in 1830 her pupil Louis-Philippe ascend the throne.

Pamela

In 1786, when I was twelve years old, Maman took us to England – that is, Henriette and myself and poor Mademoiselle, the elder surviving twin daughter of the Duchesse de Chartres, whom my mother says she loves so much (but whom she hates in reality, for I have learned to look behind the mask worn night and day by the Comtesse de Genlis). She wishes the wife of Philippe dead, yet she wears her ring – 'You will never know how much I love you,' the mother of Maman's pupils has inscribed there, and Félicité has responded in kind. I am beginning to understand the rivalry felt by women who both love the same man, and even cherish the same ambitions – though Madame de Chartres would never own to a thirst for power, she is too loyal to the King and Queen for that.

I am a prisoner and I believed I would be free. I am taken to all the palaces and grand salons: I have been the unwilling recipient of a kiss from Horace Walpole, who remarked to Maman that she had educated me to 'look very like her in the face.' I did not care for his Strawberry Hill and, if it had not been for Henriette bursting out laughing at the expression I make when I am bored, I would have stepped out of the windows with their foolish Gothic frames and gone walking in the park instead. I have seen the Court at Windsor and sat two hours while Madame de Genlis, the famous author of *Adèle et Théodore* and *Les Veillées du Château*, conversed with Miss Fanny Burney.

Why did I imagine I would find freedom in the country where Maman is so eager to prove I was born that she has approached a man of great eminence, the Lord Mansfield, to ask him to give a certificate to that effect? 'Yes, I will ensure that you see your mother. She will travel to London to attest when the certificate is prepared,' Maman said. And I dreamed, while the *grands gens* of Oxford where Madame de Genlis received her degree all stared at me as if I had come there from another planet, that Mary Sims would take me with her to the house by the grey sea where the washing would take three full days to dry, so heavy was the salt in the sheets and long shirts that flap on the line. There I would be free.

γ

I am known for playing the harp; and, wherever I go, a harp is brought so people can swoon at my beauty accompanied by heavenly music. Already, at twelve years old, I am a spectacle: 'La Belle Pamela,' Henriette says and she pretends to look serious, as if weighing me up for a prize. 'Don't imagine Maman wastes her time here – she looks for a husband already, for her little protégée,' Henriette says. 'The son of a duke – preferably a connection with a royal bastard, such as people say is your own history.'

I didn't listen to any of the teasing. I waited and waited for Mary Sims. She never came. 'I asked Monsieur Forth to bring her to London,' Maman says, and when she is impatient she raps her fingers, which are loaded with gems, across her writing desk, a portable box she takes everywhere, with knife and fork and glass for a picnic, as well as ink and quill pens inside. I can hear the rapping now, and see the English rain as it comes down in Portland Place, in the great mansion Papa bought, for he loves England. I would also, if I could, leave the special occasions Madame makes me attend and go home to the green hills and the swans and the ruin of St Catherine's Chapel which stands on the hill above Abbotsbury like a reminder of all I have lost in my strange, uncertain life.

So the visit goes on. Maman pretends that Mary Sims refuses to travel up to London because Monsieur Forth has been instructed not to bring her in luxury. I doubt this is the reason; but I think Maman will lose much through her meanness; if she loves me, and if she truly believes this certificate of my English birth will be of use to her, then she should have permitted a poor washerwoman to travel in comfort. Now I feel my mother will never come, and I am surrounded by uncertainty again – but no sooner have I become re-acclimatised to my invalid existence than Madame announces one day at breakfast that the certificate is signed, and has been produced by Lord Mansfield. 'What happened to Mrs Sims?' Félicité repeats after me, as if surprised by my question. 'Why, she has other children to get home to, Pamela. Monsieur Forth packed her back down to Bournemouth on the coach. She is well cared for. The Reverend Jeans – you will remember him at the Embassy in Paris when we visited Nathaniel, Monsieur Forth, there – is a native of Christchurch. He does not forget Mary Sims. He it was who found you, much to my everlasting happiness.'

So it was that my dreams of escape ended. Maman, Henriette, Mademoiselle and the one they all stare at as they do at the freaks in the grounds of the Palais Royal – that is, myself, La Belle Pamela, the possessor of a beauty they tell me is already so rare that my keeper Madame de Genlis can take me anywhere in the world and gain admiration for having discovered me (as the saying goes) – all went yesterday to the House of Commons, where a special performance of *Hamlet* was staged in our honour. Tomorrow we return to France. The harp will stand in the salon where I am painted, along with Maman, Henriette and Mademoiselle. If there is to be another way of life – a life where all are free – then I will gladly stay in France and fight for it.

Pamela

For now I must tell myself that I am fortunate to have lost my mother Mary Sims to a life in which I can no longer act the part required of me. My destiny must lie in Paris, with those who struggle to be free.

Little Pam

I had heard that the beauty of my mother Pamela, and her position at the Court of the prince who would, when the time came, choose the name Egalité to show his belief in the rule of the people of France, had made her popular to the point of becoming famous; what I had not understood until the last weeks before her death was the extent of her loyalty to Philippe, both as her father and as a believer in the Revolution right up to the day he was taken off to the guillotine himself. When she spoke to me of the event which could be said to have started the Revolution, the riot at the Reveillon wallpaper factory, I felt myself in the crowds, the dying and the injured lying around me in the Faubourg Saint Antoine; when she told me of the sacrifices made by the Duc d'Orléans to alleviate the terrible poverty of the masses, I saw the Palais Royal as she described it, stripped of the magnificent paintings the great family of Orléans had accumulated over the centuries and the proceeds handed out to those suffering

in the famine. I hated the Queen, Marie Antoinette, as
Madame de Genlis and the Duc d'Orléans had loathed
her; I suffered, in those moments when Pamela, propped
on her pillow, felt once again the intense joy and
anguish of those times. Yet I knew, and could not bring
myself to remind her, of the fact that the Duc d'Orléans
had given a great ball in that same season of starvation
and despair to celebrate his new silver service, made to
order by the acclaimed English silversmith, Arthur. Had
she not told me of those glittering festivities in the past?
I confess I found it hard to understand my mother at
these times, for she appeared half in love with equality
and Revolution while the other half was still anchored
in the Ancien Régime – like her different-coloured eyes,
perhaps, which gazed out on a country painted in two
different colours.

It was hard for me, also, to envisage the effect of
such fame on an orphan brought from an English village
and lacking any title or true position of her own. What
can it have been, to be acclaimed by a mob in the
gardens of the Palais Royal crying 'Pamela for Queen'?
And did this in fact take place? (For my mother had a
modesty which never deserted her: 'I was mistaken for
the dashing Théorigne de Mericourt,' Pamela said,
sinking back in the half-light which came in only a few
hours each day from the street. 'She had a scarlet outfit
and wore black feathers in her hat. On one occasion
Maman dressed me like that and I was mistaken for her.
I was never considered the future people's Queen.')

By the time these stories came out, I was old enough to know my protestations as a child – 'They did, Mama! Everyone wanted you as their Queen!' – were as childishly loyal as my mother's had been on the subject of Philippe, right to the end of her life. The Revolutionary spirit, which seemed to breed whenever this charming young woman was on the scene, had preserved her, possibly, in the beliefs and certainties of her early years; but for me, her daughter, too much has passed in that brief span since I was small to give faith to any other than the God in whom I place my trust. My mother, so I believe, celebrates to her dying day the excitement of having been present at the birth of a new world. And, as I hear her memories that come in with the dim light, the smell of frying and the shouts of the women as they jostle in the poor streets beyond the hotel window, I become her small daughter again. I am in Dublin, waiting for my own father, the leader of the Irish rebels, to return from his latest struggle with those who rule our sad country, and Pamela's stories are as clear and real as if they had been my own.

'I was woken,' my mother says, 'when it was still evening. I had been put to bed early; I never knew why. My father had been dining with the Scotchwoman, Grace Elliott. He told me to get up quickly and help him put on his disguise. We were going to march on Versailles, he said. So I went with him, out to meet the poissardes.'

Pamela

I had known the language of the fish
women, the market people who mixed their words with
earth and spat them back at the rich who took their
bread and the bakers who held back their supplies, since
I had been brought as a child to the place where every
café and booth shouted a delighted response to their
bawdy sketches and songs. The Duc d'Orléans – whom
the poissardes would never have seen as my father; there
was no sense of family, as we would see it, among these
people, only the muscle of need and the power of a tribe
– had a theatre in the grounds of the Palais Royal,
where young aristocrats mixed with the traders, and
their rough, salty language was spoken on stage, the
jokes and contempt of the poor of Paris lapped up by
the nobility. Here, I used to sit with Papa and with the
man I saw on that fateful evening, as he crossed the
gardens and, seeing us together, smiled, bowed and paid
me his compliments which had tips as sharp and
pointed as a sword. If Laclos had wanted, he could have

taken me from my innocent life at Belle-Chasse and plunged me in a world a hundred times more decadent than I had already seen in this enclave of vice, as the respectable people of Paris saw the Palais Royal and its inhabitants. It was a measure of the strength of the tie which had grown between the writer and nobleman, and Philippe Duc d'Orléans, that I was left unmolested by that monster. My poor Papa would do anything for him, but I believe also that his love for me was so great that the demands of the author of *Les Liaisons Dangereuses* for time alone with La Belle Pamela were inevitably refused. Besides, on that evening of October 4th, 1789, he had other matters on his mind.

Paris was alive that evening. I know I felt as if I had woken up for the first time, at the age of fifteen, to all the prospects which lay before me. I was aware, from the lights on the river, these reflected from the lamps erected in the garden where all was possible – Revolution, wit, repartee, the jostling of rich and poor together, the wine and zeal of a new world of equality and liberty in the making – that the evening had scarcely begun. Along with the promise in the blue hour brought by the fading of day and the lighting of a thousand candles in the cafés and meeting houses of the grounds belonging to our beautiful Palais came an underswell, a sense that the whole city joined us now in our terrible expectations. And as I followed my father I was aware, too, I must admit, of as many glances following me in turn as candles flickering to life in the low windows of buildings where the new beliefs and precepts were declaimed. These were countered by the blunt, half-loathing, half-loving wit of the poissardes, and it was at such a moment, when the whole place was in uproar, and the lights on the river shone like diamonds in Marie Antoinette's necklace, that we knew the future had now found the moment to enter our present. Paris rose; and the people rose with the city, as silent and menacing in their great tumult as a herd of deer when it crosses the floor of the forest. For, under the rumble of the distant noise, the quiet of a new resolve could now be heard.

We went in a cabriolet to Meudon, to the house of the Scotchwoman Grace Elliott. No one recognised the Duc d'Orléans, who sat well back in the carriage, as we went; and I realised this journey was the most important we had taken together, for Philippe, who was then at the height of his popularity, liked generally to look out at the crowds. Some shouted, 'Vive Orléans,' even though they had no idea their hero travelled amongst them; and I have often thought that Laclos, who had something of a magician's ability to render himself and those with him invisible, was responsible for our anonymous passage to Meudon on that night. That my dear Papa, misguidedly as I now believe, wished, when seen the next time in public, to be in quite a different guise had not at all occurred to me.

$\mathcal{Y}$

I had done all I could over past years to remove the influence of Grace Elliott on Monseigneur, the prince whose mistress she had been. Henriette, with much pulling of faces and sucking in of her waist, as if trying to emulate the woman considered the most beautiful in the realm, had informed me of this liaison when I was still a child at Maman's school, retiring to bed even before the early dances were over and attempting so hard to please the Comtesse de Genlis that I was in the habit of falling sobbing to my knees for even the slightest peccadillo, such as losing a pair of Madame's sewing scissors. I hadn't known how to accept the news of the Duc's infidelity to the woman who had charge of his children (I somehow evaded the thought of Madame de Chartres, their real mother and Papa's wife), and I refused at first to believe the man who stood for a new, Revolutionary France could be capable of a crime as sordid and contemptible as adultery.

'That's not all,' Henriette said. We were in her upstairs room at the convent and two nuns walked below us in the arcade newly built to connect the pupils with the convent itself. It must have been the first time I wondered at a man like Choderlos de Laclos, or the ugly-faced M. Mirabeau, being permitted into these sanctified surroundings. I knew somehow that there were many love affairs, 'adventures', as I'd heard Maman refer to the romantic escapades of these pretty women. I knew she tried to guard me from becoming one such myself, as I was often compared with Lady

Hamilton, whose attitudes were famous all through Europe. But I had not doubted the absolute loyalty of Philippe Duc d'Orléans to the woman who was considered by all to be my actual mother, and who liked those she reared to see her as their own mother as well.

'I feel sorry for poor M. de Genlis,' Henriette had gone on, in that room I shall connect forever with an ending to my innocence, the clematis outside rampant with May flowers and the nuns walking in their black robes as if spring could no longer touch their hearts. 'He found happiness with that lovely woman Madame de Buffon – her father-in-law brings us the specimens of plants and the frogs we dissect in our lessons on science, you know whom I mean, Pamela – and they could be seen together wherever you went, so I knew from a cousin of my mother's anyway.'

It was some years later that I heard the next instalment. I was still afraid of Henriette when she acted the grown-up in this way, and I knew I should still be alarmed by her revelations. At the same time I felt anxious, I suppose, at any possible threat to my own security, tenuous as it was in this royal household where everyone but myself had a recognisable position. Even my younger sister Hermine – whom Henriette secretly teased, taunting her with the lack of the beauty with which I had been both blessed and cursed – was settled with Madame de Laowestine, the daughter of Madame de Genlis. She would learn the ways of motherhood by taking care of little Hermine, so our Maman said. I had no wish to hear of further upheavals in the family. But I knew Henriette would tell me what I must fear; and it was shortly before the night of the great March that she looked at me in mock astonishment and answered my clumsy questions on the amorous affairs of my father.

'Why, the Duc has fallen madly in love with Madame de Buffon,' Henriette replied. 'He takes her to the theatre every night; they go for drives each afternoon in his curricle.'

It would be hard to describe my feelings on hearing this. I knew that Madame de Buffon's politics were very similar to those of my father, and so I was relieved in one way that he would no longer be influenced by the Englishwoman Grace Elliott. For Grace was a courtesan, and this I had known and regretted ever since Papa started taking me on his visits to her elegant little house in the woods at Meudon: she revered princes and rich men – she loved power, in short; and her main aim, when Philippe came to call there, was to bring him together with the King and Queen again, to put him on the side of all he had taught me to despise and wish out of the way in the shape of the monarchy. Madame de Buffon would do the very opposite, it was true, but I feared, in my possessive way, that I would lose the regard and friendship of Philippe d'Orléans once he had found true happiness and understanding with one whose beliefs mirrored his. I was, in fact, thinking only of myself and of a future without the presence of the man I loved above all others when Henriette started her giggling again and tossed her hair, which was more frizzed than usual on this damp September day.

'Don't look so serious,' said this Mademoiselle de Sercey, this friend who pretended to know everything and was in fact too ignorant to understand the meaning of the new ideas that Maman teaches at her school at Belle-Chasse. (I do not complain, as Henriette does, at having to eke out the soup with water and crumble our bread into the bowl, for I know I am engaged in learning the new thinking that will benefit all of mankind.)

'I am sorry for M. de Genlis, that is all,' says Henriette, seeing me turn from the window that looks out on clematis now dying in the autumn sun, brown and severe as the vine the nuns have trained over the convent portal. 'He is twice cuckolded by Monseigneur, who took both his mistress and his wife. However, the beautiful Grace Elliott still keeps her sway over M. d'Orléans, we hear. She is ever accommodating, the Scotchwoman whose daughter by the King of England is, they say, very plain. But she has less influence on the Duc than she had before; and this, Pamela, you will be happy to hear.'

Little Pam

And so,' my mother said, 'it was for me to decide on my father's conduct that night. Should he join the women of Paris, the women who came in their thousands with their knives and pitchforks to demand bread of the King and his wicked Queen; should he walk with them, disguised as a poissarde, or would he lose his popularity if he did so? I was appealed to: the other women who dominated him would have torn him apart if he had listened to their separate advice. I am not sure, even now, that I did the right thing on that fateful night.'

When I was small, and tucked up by the fire at Blackrock, the house my father loved, by the sea outside Dublin, I would ask again and again for the story of the march on Versailles. How Pamela had gone to the Duc d'Orléans, saying she believed her Papa should join the market women – he was, after all, a true believer in democracy, and they would love him all the more for walking with them in the autumn storms – and how he had embraced her, crying a little at the sincerity of her desire to have him loved by all the poor people of Paris.

'The contents of his famous picture gallery at the Palais Royal had been sold and the bread given to the midwives and to the poor,' my mother said; and we would sit a while in silence in the drawing room of that elegant small house, knowing as she spoke that Ireland starved as France once had, and that my own father, the leader of the rebels, protested as the Duc d'Orléans had once done, and fought on the behalf of the miserable and the poor. 'So I was sent down to the kitchens in the house of Grace Elliott to find a dress for my father to wear. The cook was a Jacobin; she helped me; and when Madame de Buffon came knocking on the door, we slipped together up the back stairs to the room where the Duc waited for us in some impatience. Yes, I was the one who laced the First Prince of the Blood into the stained skirts and ripped bodice of a gown long ago discarded by the cook. I remember that his feet stuck out, like a clown in the pantomime, under the obvious disguise. M. de Laclos, with his narrow shoulders, looked better in his false attire. His blue eyes shone that night, I remember this also – and the lovely Mrs Elliott gazed at him as if she was for the first time really afraid of what this cold, calculating man could do to the man she loved: a man, after all, who preferred pleasure to the Revolution, for all his talk and appearance of ambition. I think, on that evening, I liked Grace Elliott, despite the fact she was a royalist to the last – I understood that she wanted to save Papa from himself, and that Madame de Buffon, who had the Revolutionary fever in her veins, cared much less for what could happen to him.'

'So it was raining,' I would say sleepily, on those long nights when you could hear the sea beyond the garden at Blackrock, and when no one ever knew whether the sound of English soldiers marching was hidden under the crash of the waves. 'And you set out, carried by the women who advanced on Versailles.'

'Yes,' my mother says – and now, as she leans forward in bed in the undistinguished hotel where her mother, the Marquise de Sillery, Madame de Genlis (for was that not, after all, the tie?), has permitted her once-adored daughter to end her days, I see her relive the extraordinary occasion of the fishwomen's assault on the King's great Palace: the rain, the glasses of free wine handed out, the speeches, and the rush on the Queen's chambers, the nearness of the assassination of the woman all France had learned to hate. 'I was appalled at the poverty of the poissarde women, many of whom were almost naked,' my mother goes on, 'but at least I had seen such people, I had met them at the Palais Royal. For the Dauphin and for the courtiers at Versailles, the appearance of the women came as a shock.'

When the story was over, I would already have fallen asleep, and the ending would have to be retold the next day: the heads of the royal bodyguard held aloft on pikes, the coming out on to the balcony of the King, and then, alone and summoning all the dignity she could find, Marie Antoinette. The roar from the crowd, as General Lafayette stooped to kiss the Queen's hand. Their rush to a house in Passy and their own appearance on the balcony there: 'Yes, the Duc had changed to being a man again,' my mother said, laughing, 'and this time I had to pin the great tricolour cockade on his hat. In the end we could only secure it with a steel buckle. The red, white and blue were the Orléans colours, you know. I thought – and I believe Maman thought on the day the King and Queen were brought into Paris by Lafayette and came in their carriages beneath our balcony in Passy – that Orléans would be created Regent, or even crowned King.'

And Grace? She gave firm evidence when questioned that the Duc had breakfasted at her house; it was understood that he had spent the night with his long-time mistress and no more was said. 'But I – ' says my mother, who can confide these matters to me now, for I had been too young in Ireland for talk of love and of the women who made poor Philippe dance like a puppet at their varying commands, those women, such as Félicité de Genlis, Agnes de Buffon, Grace Elliott and the Duchesse herself, before a final argument over the scheming Madame de Genlis separated husband and wife, 'I knew the Duc d'Orléans did not spend the night at the house of Grace Elliott. She kept all twenty candles in her bedchamber burning all night, to deceive those who came to hunt him – so the cook told me. And a very pretty bedchamber it was – like the other rooms it was bordered with a ravishing pattern of roses on a black background and the walls were a delightful sea green, which went very well with the Englishwoman's complexion.' And at that, my mother closes her eyes. A bell from the church of Ste Marguerite sounds the hour; it is time for me to creep out.

Y

These were the fleeting images my mother gave me: the time at Belle-Chasse when coming in unexpectedly on a meeting between Philippe, Félicité and Mirabeau, she was told to stay as quiet as a mouse until they had shown M. Petion, the other conspirator present, to the door. Madame de Genlis, so Pamela would say with the deprecating, half-quizzical expression she assumed when talking of her mother, would be wearing on this occasion the brooch she loved to flaunt after the fall of the Bastille – 'Everyone said we were taken to see that happen,' so Pamela said, and again she laughed. I was reminded, at those times, of her gaiety when I myself was a child – until, of course, the dreadful day when I could no longer stay with my mother, and had to leave Paris. The music from the barrel organ filled the street; it was crude and loud and I wept all the way to the grey sea, the boat, the grim houses of Calais.

'Everyone in the cafés and theatres at the Palais Royal swore they had seen us, Madame de Genlis and her royal pupils, her little adopted daughter as always one of the crowd. We were reported standing on the balcony of the house of M. Beaumarchais, the great dramatist, to watch the fortress of the Bastille as it fell. But we did not: Madame de Genlis was far too protective of the child she hoped to see one day on the throne, Louis-Philippe d'Or-léans, to allow him to go into danger. She knew already, I believe, that my father, the man in whom she had placed all her hopes, might renounce his ambitions at the last moment and, of course, she was right: from some fatal flaw in his character he would manoeuvre himself into losing France, along with the love of the people, and finally he would lose his head, too.' And here my mother would fall silent.

'It was after we all stood together and watched the royal family go past on their way from Versailles to the Tuileries, on that October day I shall never forget,' Pamela would finish, 'that the Duc lost his popularity. He was advised to flee to England: things were bad by then and it was thought that his life was in danger; and the people despised him, the man they would have accepted as king, for slipping away.'

So I sat and saw again the pictures which neither grew nor became smaller or more dim as Pamela's life flickered before her on the walls of the first floor bedroom of the Hotel Danube. I knew the story of her mother's famous brooch: that it consisted of a stone from the Bastille, set in diamonds and garnished with the tricolor gems her lover Philippe must have commanded to be placed around this relic from the prison fortress: rubies, sapphires and more diamonds, the red, white and blue of the Revolutionary colours. I felt, when I heard the stories, on those afternoons of a dying year, the church bells muffled in the falling of the rain outside, that I could see Madame de Genlis, who never permitted herself to be known as Pamela's true mother; and I heard in my imagination the orchestra as it played *Ça Ira* – 'for no one other than Maman,' Pamela said, 'could make a quadrille from *Ça Ira*. The Orléans children and their friends would all dance to the tune.' At those times Pamela spoke more in admiration than in sadness. 'Madame de Genlis would be standing at the top of the stairs, in her dress of tricolor, and everyone was at her feet. Even when we were ourselves in great danger, her resourcefulness saved us from a terrible fate.'

I know the story: I see the carriage stopped in the country village some leagues outside Paris, and I hear the angry peasants shout that the party inside contained the Queen. 'They thought I was the daughter of the King, Madame Royale,' Pamela said. 'And little Louis-Philippe they mistook for the Dauphin. We were dragged from the carriage – we took refuge in the house of a man who had worked at Sillery for Maman's husband; and the mob broke through, right into the garden. And what did they find there? Do you remember, when we used to play that game in the house by the sea in Ireland, Pam? And how I told you it was a game that had saved my life? How clever Maman was:

how astonished the crowd became, when they saw our innocent pursuit there.'

'Yes,' I say; and I know this is one of my mother's last memories of childhood before her life changed forever. 'You were playing Puss-in-the-Corner,' I put in. 'The crowd was filled with remorse. They accompanied you on the road back to Paris. And then – '

'And after that it became too dangerous for us to stay in France,' Pamela says, and I know by the tender silence she falls into that she remembers the safety of finding, as she did, the man she was to marry and to love, in the midst of all that danger.

'So you went to England,' I say.

Y

My mother remembers that there was a crowd at the Louvre at the beginning of October 1791, and I see from her disparaging, almost dismissive way of treating the subject that she is ashamed of the pride she must have felt then in her extraordinary beauty. For while the Revolution swept relentlessly on, and the violence and hatred of the people for the royal family and the aristocrats grew, the esteemed Governor of the Orléans children and her adopted daughter Pamela were able to visit the exhibition of the painter Giroust and to receive the plaudits of all those waiting for the appearance of the three famous women: Madame de Genlis, Mademoiselle d'Orléans and Pamela Sims, considered the illegitimate daughter of Madame de Genlis and the Duc d'Orléans.

The crowd is well pleased with what it sees, both within the walls of the Louvre and in the courtyard outside. A wave of applause sounds as far as the Temple, where the King and Queen are immured; and Camille Desmoulins, pausing for his meeting with friends at Foy's, his old haunt at the Palais Royal, stands still for a second to listen to the acclaim for the woman who has brought the Orléans faction to prominence, Citoyenne Brulart-Genlis-Sillery. He saunters to the Louvre, to observe the beauty of Pamela, which is by now so well known that grown men affect to weep when afforded a glimpse of the humble girl brought over, as Citoyenne Brulart insists, from a village in England. He finds all three women are pausing to acknowledge the clapping and calls, and he sees they all wear the red cap of liberty. How well Pamela's headgear becomes her! How perfect her coiffure, under the bonnet rouge! And how Madame de Genlis sparkles, with her brooch, *Liberté* in diamonds inscribed over the precious stones, pinned to her bosom! They appear the conquerors of this glorious Revolution; yet, as Desmoulins and his associates know, they must flee the country if they are to find safety. Heads as well as those well-modelled caps of liberty will sooner or later fall under the guillotine's blade if they do not.

And the picture inside the august walls of the Louvre? 'You never could imagine,' Pamela says; and, as she leans forward to demonstrate her pose in that portrait of a banished age, it is possible for a moment to rediscover her beauty: the nose straight, the eyes black and a dark stormy grey, the perfect angle of the neck seeming to have been dictated by an artist and copied by nature for the delectation of the spectator. 'You never could believe the atrocities which were taking place all over France, at the time *The Harp Lesson* went on show. It was a world still in which most people wanted to place their trust, if only the King could understand their needs – a world where appearances counted for everything. But, you know, for all the Revolutionary beliefs Maman put forward, no one represented the Ancien Régime, its deceits and its belief in putting on a face to spite the cruelties of life, more than she.'

Always a harp, so I think when I try to imagine the world of my mother when young – the carrier, as it must have appeared to all who knew her, of the disease of change, unrest, riot and death. There is always a harp playing somewhere in the life of La Belle Pamela. And here, in the Giroust portrait, she stands as commanding as a goddess – a goddess of the music of the days of *douceur de vivre*, before the kingdom of France was cut down and set up again on the bloody scaffold in the Place de La Révolution. She holds the sheets of music that her young fellow pupil, the Princesse d'Orléans, must learn to read. The child's plump fingers stretch out across the strings of the tall, ornately carved harp. Madame de Genlis – in a straw hat as tall as a spun sugar cake, trimmed with an abundance of satin ribbon and tied under her chin (so different from the cap of liberty and, for a woman of a certain age, more becoming) – is portrayed as smaller, younger and prettier than her adopted daughter Pamela. The artist knows how to please this Marquise de Sillery, whom you would never, in the mock-classical surroundings in which the women stand, address as Citoyenne Brulart. But he has been unable to prevent himself, in the last resource, from painting Pamela as a beauty; and for this reason, perhaps, he has shown her mother, the celebrated author and educationalist, as absurdly young.

'It was just before we left for England,' Pamela says. 'And the strange part was that I saw myself in the portrait in the Louvre – and then in England it seemed people saw me as I was, but differently; they saw in me another, a woman they said I exactly resembled. And both the men who loved me saw the other woman, whom they had been in love with, too, when they first met me. But what I remember most, I have to say, is how poor we were, in London; how cold it was, and how Mademoiselle snatched the blanket from me, so I shivered all night long. It was a small house, miserable in comparison with Papa's old mansion in Portland Place. We were poor; and Maman said we would have to live very carefully; but one hundred louis d'or were gone by the end of our first few weeks there and she was hard pressed to get any more.'

Y

As I tell this story, to my grandchildren and great-grand-children, I think of the coincidence that haunted my mother's life and, as they provide a setting not unlike the fairy tales you love to hear, I shall pause in England with Pamela. You may wonder whether she would have done better to stay there or to return to France. You will remember the story related by the Duc – he who kept his cows in a Paris mansion – of a spirited old lady, Madame de Crequy, and her memoir containing the story of two beautiful young men who exactly resembled each other: the first dying before there was time for our heroine to declare her passion; and the second, seen years later as a guard at Versailles, causing the still-lovely young woman of Madame de Crequy's tale to commit the most heinous sin known at Court, which was to faint in the presence of the King. In this case, Louis XIV and his Queen were witnesses to our heroine's loss of consciousness on seeing the double of the prospective husband she had lost years before. Indeed, not long after the discovery that the paragon of good looks and virtue glimpsed at Versailles had been the illegitimate half-brother of her dead fiancé, the ravishing protagonist of this sad story herself died.

I remind you of this improbable and romantic episode because it illustrates perfectly the impossibilities and restrictions of the pre-Revolutionary age in which Pamela was reared – nourished as she was by the writings of Jean-Jacques Rousseau and educated by the one teacher in whom, despite her life of scandal, all the best people believed. Superstition abounded – tales of doubles, of babies substituted at birth, of identical twins separated and then magically reunited, formed a large part of the popular imagination. Pamela, who was childish and simple always, to the point of unquestioning loyalty, must have believed from an early age in occult powers – she had her own beauty, after all, as an example of the effect on people a set of features may produce; and her different-coloured eyes, so often referred to in the letters and journals of the period, were thought to indicate a mixed birth of no little significance. Unlike the heroine of Madame Crequy's memoir, however, Pamela had no king to make obeisance to; and the fact that her admirers jeered at monarchy and fought for a Republic made this Revolutionary heroine all the more fascinating to those who fell under her spell. Also, the doubles in question were not, as in the tale recounted by the ancient Marquise, males unconscious of each other's existence by reason of their birth. In the case of Pamela's romantic story, it was the fêted young beauty from Paris who found herself the double of an English belle as talented and delightful as herself – Elizabeth Linley, wife of the playwright Richard Brinsley Sheridan. You will have seen her portrait, painted by George Romney as St Cecilia, patron saint of music. And it is in England, when the astute and resourceful Madame de Genlis took Mademoiselle d'Orléans, Henriette de Sercey, Pamela and her own five-year-old-granddaughter away from the country where they would find themselves in danger, that this part of the story begins.

You should know that Sheridan had lost his wife three months before the arrival of Pamela on the shores of her own country. (Madame de Genlis, despite all the rumours to the effect that she brought her 'daughter with Orléans, Miss Pamela Capet' in train to England, was fervent in her protestations that the subject of *The Harp Lesson* was English and the child of a Mrs Mary Sims.) What Pamela found was a romance fashioned to be played out as a drama. The first act begins with Sheridan inconsolable at the loss of his wife. Elizabeth Linley had been, it was true, the lover of the handsome young Edward Fitzgerald: they had a child together and – as these tales always have it – were deeply in love, but the death from consumption of the unusually beautiful and gifted young woman devastated the dramatist, and he lived on alone in the house by the Thames at Isleworth where he and Elizabeth had lived happily together.

Yes, Pamela is taken to meet Mr Sheridan by the poet Robert Southey, he who has been so taken by her beauty that he writes later of the certainty that he will never forget the perfection of Pamela's face (Madame de Genlis he has forgotten already).

Pamela so closely resembles Elizabeth that Richard Brinsley Sheridan proposes immediately.

But, as Pamela accepts – and she does, as if she knows herself only another version of the dead woman,

as if a double has as little control over her or his life
as the young man born to be no more than a guard at
the Court of Louis XIV had over his – there comes a
letter to Madame de Genlis from the Duc d'Orléans,
demanding his daughter Mademoiselle is returned to
France. Poor little Mademoiselle, Marie-Adelaide Capet
as she now must be known, is fifteen years old and has
been labelled an emigrée. Why is she kept in England,
when she could be prosecuted for treason if she does not
return at once?

Despite the comic efforts of Mr Sheridan to keep his
new passion at his side – the coachmen are bribed to
gallop along a road in the opposite direction to Dover:
the hoax so alarms Madame de Genlis that she and her
party stay another four weeks at Isleworth before
setting out again – Madame de Genlis finally departs. It
is 1792 and a year has gone by, in England, since their
arrival. Pamela weeps, for she has fallen in love with
Sheridan. Henriette, sketching and painting as she fills
her days – she records Fox, and the great Thomas Paine,
and makes a pretty miniature for Pamela and her
mother to send, after their visit to Wales, to the famous
lesbian Ladies of Llangollen, Lady Eleanor Butler and
Sarah Ponsonby – looks on her friend's great romance
with some scepticism. For she has heard Madame de
Genlis making enquiries on the subject of a young man
who might be considered a good deal more suitable as a
husband for Pamela. He is none other than Edward
Fitzgerald, former lover of the sadly deceased Elizabeth

Brinsley Sheridan. And, as in all the very best true romances, Elizabeth is recorded as having begged her darling Edward, when the first news was recorded of the expected appearance in England of the strikingly similar and beautiful Pamela, to wed her once she herself is dead. So the pact was made, if not in heaven, then in the novel-style of the day. Edward, Lord and Insurrectionary, Leader of the rebel Irish against the British Crown, promises his Elizabeth that he will do as she asks him, and she fades away in his arms.

After a choppy crossing, the little party, guided by Citoyenne Brulard – formerly Madame de Genlis – arrives in France. A note comes from Philippe Egalité, formerly Duc d'Orléans. Madame is handed it at Calais. They must go no further: Paris is too dangerous now. But the people of Calais shout in rapture at the sight of Mademoiselle – *Orléans! Orléans!*

'I simply cannot imagine,' my mother says when she goes back to those days of doubles and countermanded journeys, and horses galloping away from their destinations, 'I cannot think where Maman could have found the strength, on the day after she insisted on taking us all to Paris, whatever Papa might say, to go to the theatre.'

'To the theatre?' I say, as if I have never heard the story of my parents' first meeting before.

'Yes, and we had only been given two days to leave France once more, as Mademoiselle was in danger of instant arrest. We were told we must go to Tournai, in Belgium. Maman had to get passports and make all the arrangements for our travel. All the same, she found time to procure a box at the Feydeau opera in Paris. Somehow Lord Edward happened to be at White's Hotel – it was a hotbed for revolutionaries at that point – with his friend John Reid. It happened that Mr Reid also wanted to take in *Lodoiska* and he procured a box as well.'

'You don't think Madame de Genlis had a hand in ensuring Mr Reid and Lord Edward attended the opera that night?' I ask my mother. I know she heard the teasing note in my voice but I make sure not to catch her eye.

'What can you mean, Pam?' she said. 'It was the purest coincidence. Lord Edward had declined to meet us in England, it turned out, because he couldn't abide bluestockings.'

'But he came to like Madame de Genlis in the end,' I pressed her.

'Oh yes,' came Pamela's slow reply, as she stares past the end of the bed in the small room, the peignoir hung on the doorknob, the plain mantelpiece where the tiny oval miniatures stand in their glass box on a background of crushed velvet: Lord Edward, painted in Ireland, Madame de Genlis, and Pamela in her bonnet rouge. 'I believe he did come to like her – though I, of course, found another mother, as powerful and commanding as Maman – Edward's mother Emily, who wished to take over the lives of her "sweet little Pamela" and the children.'

But I begged Pamela to leave the subject of Lord Edward's mother for a while, as I conjured up in turn the opera house on the Rue Feydeau, on the evening of 22 November 1792, when the handsome young man, recently returned from fighting in America and now prepared to save his beloved Ireland from tyranny, looked along the tier of boxes in the interval and saw a beautiful girl there. Then, as the perfect face of Elizabeth Linley, in the shape of Pamela, fades with the going down of the lights and the music of *Lodoiska* starts up once more, the scene vanishes and I am alone with Pamela, her glass of milk and the last crumbs of the chocolate profiterole one of her old admirers, the Duc de Force, has been kind enough to send in today.

'After meeting in the theatre that night,' I say, 'Madame de Genlis invited Lord Edward to supper the following evening.'

'Yes,' Pamela says, 'at Belle-Chasse.'

Y

You must imagine the scene, little Pamela who is not yet born, and who will need to know of the meeting and love between her great-grandmother La Belle Pamela and the dashing young man in a red cravat, an Irish aristocrat who insists that he is a citizen, not a lord.

The candles are lit in the blue salon where Madame de Genlis has so successfully and secretly entertained those from whom she, along with the children of the

Duc d'Orléans, must now flee for their lives: Mirabeau, Petion, Barère, Laclos. The table is laid, and adorned with sprigs of yew and Christmas roses, for the dreadful year 1793 is about to give way to another year which will prove even more bloodthirsty and terrifying than this one.

But no one thinks of this. Pamela, who looks across shyly at her new suitor, is as pale as the garlands of winter blooms. Edward, handsome and ruddy in his velvet coat, gazes back at this desirable emblem of Revolution, La Belle Pamela, and they fall in love.

Pamela

I came across the Channel the first time with Monsieur Forth, the Sheep as I thought of him; and now, if I ask my new husband what has happened to that procurer for the Duc d'Orléans, a pompous, foolish but good-natured man, I receive only the reply that I should not think any more of what has happened in France. I shall be Irish now, and my new mother Emily, who is English, will ensure that I am loved in the country where I remember most of all as a child the swans, and a bank of pebbles made tall and strong by the sea. Emily will take care of me and I will love her and Edward's sisters in return. My past visits to England with Madame de Genlis will count for nothing in my memory soon, Edward says; and then he looks sad, as if his own memories of the woman he loved there are bound to return to him as soon as he arrives. My hopes are for Ireland, and the house on the sea at Blackrock, where there are roses and honeysuckle and where his mother, who will love me so much, has made a book-room which contains all the works of dear Maman. I shall be happy; I shall knit a cap for the child Henriette told me will come once I am settled in my new country.

But I know Edward thinks of France, and he believes the French will save his beloved Ireland, just as he prays his love for me will carry away his sadness over poor Elizabeth. I have heard him speak aloud in his sleep, in the little cabin we share. Edward grew up in France, in the Château d'Aubigny, which had belonged to his great-grandmother Louise de Kerouailles. It is why his heart is as much in France as in Ireland. So why am I not to think of the country I have long seen as mine? What does Edward hide from me? What is happening to my father there? What does Edward know and refuse to tell?

Little Pam

My mother, recalling her bewilderment in the hard spring of 1793, can only fall silent when the day comes to speak of her father's treachery to the royal family. She suggests we walk in the Tuileries gardens and we do, though the sound of a child's drum and the sight of a small boy as he struts along in scarlet tunic and gold-tasselled cap alarms and saddens her all the more, as I can see. Pamela's father Philippe must appear before her, at the sound of the drum, and bring back the memory of the executions; and her son Edward, taken from her later in Ireland for his own safety, his absence mourned night and day, must take the form of the child marching before her. For this is a time when she wishes to talk of the years before I was born, or was conscious of her pain.

The flowers in the Tuileries gardens are red and yellow, and the child who makes the insistent noise vanishes down the grand steps in his scarlet and gold.

Pamela hears the drums in her memory as they roll out news of the death on the scaffold of the King; and she stands a while confused by her surroundings, for 'I was not here,' she says, 'when the King was taken to the Place de La Révolution. I was in Ireland. I knew that the courtesan Grace Elliott, whom I had never liked, had done all she could to prevent the Duc d'Orléans from voting for the death of his cousin. I liked her even less when I heard of the efforts she had made to deflect my father from his courageous action. And, I have to confess, I felt triumph at the lack of success of her urgings. That Philippe gave as his reason for signing the death warrant of King Louis his belief that the people must be sovereign of France, not a man with a heredi-tary title, seemed to me admirable. But I was still young, then – nineteen years old – and I wished to please my new husband, dear Edward, and to shock those who fell into paroxysms of grief in England and in the stately homes of the conquerors of the Irish, the old English families in that country, at the news of the King's death. They hated me, of course, for what I was. They believed that I encouraged Lord Edward in his revolutionary mania. But he was his own man, an upholder of the writings of the great Thomas Paine, long before he married me and came into the nest of traitors, as the Orléanistes came to be known.'

I listen: and as she speaks I know my mother forgets the simple gaiety she had in the days of her youth. So I ask her, in as naive a tone as possible, if she had felt later that it was wrong for Philippe to betray his own cousin, King Louis XVI of France?

My mother laughs. I see, behind the sadness and the lines which capture and destroy that perfect face, a glimpse of the old happiness she knew when she was first married – and some of the rebellious spirit she loved to show off. 'I was at a great Dublin ball on the day the announcement of the death of the King was made,' she says. 'I was all in black, you know, even down to black stockings – not mourning dress, but just to be different. Then, when the news was given out at the ball, everyone thought I had known already of the assassination, as they termed it. They never forgot that I was all in black that evening – and that I wore red ribbons in my hair . . .'

Y

All I know of the years between the marriage of my parents, Edward and Pamela, and my own birth two and a half years later, is that they were happy ones. My mother, the 'Dear Love' of her husband's sisters Lucy and Sophie, was seen as the possessor of a clever, active mind and an elegance in dress and manner which drew everyone to love her. And I felt, whenever I was given anecdotes of that time so perplexing to anyone who has ever been born, that time when they were not in the world but were about to be, that if I had appeared a little sooner I might have prevented the ill fortune, even disaster, which was to fall on the family. If I had been a part of my cherished father's life earlier, surely I could have persuaded him to leave Ireland and emigrate to America, as was strongly suggested to him, when times grew so dangerous? There would, if I had understood the situation in my first years, that is to say the years 1796 to 1798, have been plenty of opportunities for a rebel such as my father to have understood the needs of his 'sweet little wife' and their new daughter, Little Pam as I was known, rather than allow us to go widowed and fatherless all over Europe. It was with bitter thoughts such as these that I reflected on my father's self-willed destruction – but then, as my own mother Pamela's eloquent silence showed when the subject was raised, she herself lost Philippe her father, whom she adored, to the ideals in which he had always believed. She was prepared to stand by him years after his death on the same scaffold to which he had sentenced the King: should I not, when visited by sadness at the loss of my father, do the same? Lord Edward Fitzgerald was, after all, a hero for Ireland. I should be proud to live with his memory.

My real memories as a small child are of Frescati, the house at Blackrock by the sea, not far from Dublin. My mother and father both loved it there, and I believe they cared for it a great deal more than the house at Kildare we later had to move to due to the impending sale of Frescati. Edward's mother's husband Mr Ogilvie, who was a hard man according to my poor mother Pamela, had declared that the Duchess of Leinster – Emily, Edward's mother and my grandmother, who married Mr Ogilvie, the children's tutor, after the death of the Duke – visited Ireland too seldom to justify keeping on that lovely house with its mass of wild plants and the book-room where I remember, but only vaguely, Pamela sitting with her work basket on the table before her. Mr Ogilvie did not like my mother; my grandmother Emily did; but I was naturally too young then to see the dark shadow that possessive and overbearing woman cast on her son's sweet little wife – just as I had no notion that the Mr O'Connor who came to the house to talk late by the great turf fire planned to overthrow the rulers of our poor country. He cared not at all that my father risked his life for his efforts on behalf of the United Irishmen and that my mother and I, last remnants of what should have been our perfect family, might well be scattered and forgotten. I saw only the sky, as it glowed and darkened above my crib, at Blackrock or at Castletown where my aunt Louisa Connolly lived and a child could run for an hour in the cold, mournful walls without going out into the light of day, or at Leinster House, the Duke's gloomy castle in Dublin, where we never stayed long. I didn't wonder at my mother's escapades – those that caused her to be hated in her youth by the grandees who were the English in Ireland; and I understood how she must have wept at the poverty of the peasants and the cruelty of the landlords. I admired her when I heard, already separated from her in Paris when I was aged fifteen, of her rebellion against the Anglo-Irish when she was young, just married to my father and going each night to parties and balls. But I understood why she was the subject of slanders and gossip: too blatant a delight at the death of the greatly lamented King of the French would not endear her to the gentry, any more than would the proclamation of war between France and England, which came just one month after the marriage of Pamela to my father. She was soon seen as a monster by many in the country she had so hoped would love her.

$\mathcal{Y}$

Edward Fitzgerald's life had been in danger, as I was to learn while still very young, once before. Perhaps that was why the soldiers of the British and the threat of assassination meant so little to him: the memory of the day, in the American War, when he had lain bleeding to death at the battle of Eutaw Springs in Carolina, must have always remained with him. He had been only twenty-two at the time; his life was saved by a black man, Tony Small, who, on seeing the wounded soldier, had picked him up and carried him to safety where he was able to recover; since then, Tony Small had accompanied my father everywhere.

When I was born, my mother and father were in Hamburg, a free town, and were meeting with French and Irish revolutionaries – though Pamela, being seven months pregnant, was confined to the house, which my father was not. My brother, little Eddy, was two years old in that year, 1796. The fret and exhaustion of travel and, I dare say, hearing of the incendiary plans of the revolutionaries brought on my birth two months before its time. My mother was in need of a nursemaid; and Julie, who had been attached to her household in France, had married Tony Small a few months earlier. She also expected a child; and Mauricio, son of Julie and Tony Small, a mulatto of whom I became extremely fond, was my playmate when I was young.

That Julie may emerge from our story as the final betrayer of my mother's trust is a fact which must be mentioned, even if it cannot be proved.

Pamela

I wish you to know something, Little Pam, of the years, alas so brief, that fell between the time of your birth and the tragic death of your father, Lord Edward, from the wounds he suffered resisting arrest in Dublin Castle. I knew myself alone again when Edward was in hiding and far from me, as alone as I had been in the days when the one who was perhaps my true mother, Mary Sims the washerwoman, brought me up. And you will see, when I tell you of the great betrayal practised by Madame de Genlis, that I prayed to be released from her demand for love and the constant rejection which accompanied it. I knew myself abandoned, as I had been on the day Monsieur Forth came to buy me for the little French girls in their palace where everything was other than what it seemed and all the talk of equality and liberty was played out against a painted backdrop.

I became a child in the dark, cold rooms of the great house in Dublin where my husband's brother smiled

little and I was treated as a stranger. So you may understand the reasons for my lack of discretion in the week
preceding Lord Edward's capture and my wish to beg
your forgiveness for my foolish conduct, which led, so
you may come to believe, to your orphaned state and
our unhappy destiny. If I could live those days again, I
would offer my own life to prevent the maid Julie from
giving the information of Edward's whereabouts to
Mr Ogilvie on the fateful occasion of his visit to Denzil
Street in Dublin. She knew very well that it would anger
both your parents considerably if she were to give away
the secret meeting place of those brave Irishmen. Yet,
swayed by the generous sum offered by the cunning
Mr Ogilvie, she succumbed to his bribe.

You will recall, Pammy, the desire Julie always had
to start up a dressmaking business, and for herself and
Tony to find themselves independent in London. As
a Frenchwoman, she believed she had a chance of
succeeding with a venture such as this. Out of greed and
ambition she gave Mr Ogilvie the address of a publican
by the name of Moore, in Thomas Street where Lord
Edward was hiding out; it was Moore's private address.

You must know that Lord Edward acted exactly
according to his nature when he saw Mr Ogilvie on the
doorstep of his secret meeting place: he took a ring from
his finger and handed it to his stepfather, remarking that
he was too deeply committed to the insurgents with
whom he was in the process of conferring to accept the
offer extended through Mr Ogilvie on behalf of the

British Government. This was that he leave the country with his wife and child – with you, sweet little Pam – and that all the ports would be open to him if he chose to do so. The ring from Lord Edward's finger was given by Mr Ogilvie to me; and I think often of it, hoping and praying that I may wake and find myself with the ring on my finger in the book-room at Frescati, with a jug of scyllas and white narcissus on the table and Edward walking in the door to see his little Pam in her crib by the fire. But it can never be.

This disgraceful action on the maid Julie's part took place in the spring of 1798, and Lord Edward, by visiting his wife disguised as a woman, on that very night, hastened the birth pains of your mother, and caused your sister Lucy, a seven-months baby, to come into the world. I shall forever hold myself responsible for the lack of robust good health which Lucy suffered all her short life. We cannot tell, when we act injudiciously, how long and awful the reverberations over the years may turn out to be.

I remember most of all that when Sophie let in Lord Edward in his disguise, I screamed and clutched at Julie, whom I thought still to be my most loyal friend; and how, when she said I must not take such alarm, I could only reply, half-fainting, that I had fastened a woman's dress on the Duc d'Orléans when he had gone on the march with the poissardes to Versailles, and I hated to see my husband appear also in travesty. The outcome was certain to be bad. Of course I did not know then that it was she who had given Moore's address to the authority; and I believed, as we two Frenchwomen stood together in the room before she went to lead my disguised husband to our room, that she saw as I did the light in which your father and I were regarded by the English, both in their country and in Ireland, as bearers of anarchy and chaos, emissaries of the dreadful Revolution in France. The discovery of Lord Edward's illegal visit to his wife could only make matters worse. But Julie, ready to betray us as I now know, had little concern for the future of Ireland, or for your poor father.

Despite this, you have a right to learn of the very great happiness enjoyed by your parents, before Lord Edward's arrest and fatal sword wound caused your poor mother to lose him forever.

The Lodge at Kildare – after Frescati was sold and we could go there no more – was the house we came to love most in Ireland. It was small, and prettily set out with gardens and a village where the local apothecary, the excellent Mr Cummins, was happy to be called to come and join in the dancing in the evenings. The maids and other servants were invited, too, when the reading and talking of the liberation of Ireland before the turf fire was over for the night; and I know that your father and myself were considered excessively democratic in our ways, insisting we all dance a jig together.

Sometimes we would travel to spend time with relatives. Julie would be your nursemaid on visits to Lord

Edward's aunt, Lady Louisa Connolly, at Castletown –
and I would grow homesick, longing for a return to our
cosy home at Kildare. Of my husband's sisters, I loved
Lucy the most; and I thought always lovingly of his
mother, Emily Duchess of Leinster, who was by now
the wife of Mr Ogilvie. When we left Hamburg after
your birth – and there many plots were hatched, to
bring in France on the side of helping the Irish – we
stopped first in London with the Duchess, and there it
was that your brother, two-year-old little Eddy, was
taken from me and handed over to the Duchess – for
reason, it was said, of ensuring the child's safety. For it
was known by then that Lord Edward prepared for
Revolution in Ireland. But I heard the Duchess's maid
say she knew Lord Edward had promised his firstborn
to his mother to bring up, long before he married; and
I wept at being separated from my son. But, by then,
dear little Pam, I had seen only wars and uprisings, and
danger even if there was none. I saw the beheaded
corpses in the Place de la Révolution in my dreams and
a scaffold erected in Dublin, and so I was in the habit,
I suppose, of obeying the strong women who became
dictators of my life – Madame de Genlis was the first,
and then Lord Edward's mother, Emily. By the autumn
of the year you were born, 1796, we had only yourself,
little Pam, with us, having lost your brother Eddy to his
grandmother.

I often pondered the nature of Madame de Genlis-
Sillery-Brulart, as she came to be known in the Revolu-

tion, and whether, as was confided in her romances and novels, she was in fact the mother of two little girls born outside wedlock with a father who was recognisably the Duc d'Orléans. Sometimes it seemed to me that this celebrated Madame de Genlis had no real love for the young women said by everyone to be her daughters – myself, Pamela Sims, and the child they all pretended was my sister, little Hermine. Too often I found the clever and renowned educationalist Madame de Genlis cold and calculating in the extreme, and intent on preserving her reputation, for I heard her on several occasions insist to Lord Edward that the lovely girl he intended to marry was in truth the daughter of a poor washerwoman from Christchurch and not, as Lord Edward and his family undoubtedly believed, the offspring of Madame de Genlis herself with Philippe Egalité.

It was hard to know, as Madame de Genlis was out to please the eligible young man at this time, why she made this insistence on my humble English parentage. 'My angel, my adopted daughter Pamela, was born at Fogo, in Newfoundland,' she would declare, when she thought they were alone together, and I and my friend Henriette de Sercey were sorting clothes in the next room. 'Pamela lived with her mother Mary Sims near Bournemouth once the child's father, a seal hunter by the name of William Brixey, brought mother and daughter back from Newfoundland,' Madame de Genlis said. 'In England, in the small village of Christchurch,

Pamela spent her first six years until Monsieur Forth – commissioned by His Royal Highness the Duc d'Orléans (then Chartres) to procure an English girl who would speak in her own tongue to his twin daughters – found the adorable child and brought her, along with a fine mare, to Paris.'

I have no notion of how my dear Edward took all this, but I do know that an odd occurrence in London, directly after our marriage, did possibly go some way to substantiating the avowal of Madame de Genlis that she was not, and never could have been, my mother. If this one day proves to be the case, you must, dear Pammy, forfeit your claim to royal blood; but, seeing your pity for the oppression of the Irish, and your loyalty to your friends and Fitzgerald cousins, I very much doubt that you would regret the discovery that Philippe Duc d'Orléans had not in fact been your mother's father. You would be relieved, I suspect, to learn that the man who betrayed the King of France – and who had done so in the fervent hope of saving his own life – was no tie. For myself, I loved him as my father. The following episode may cause you to reconsider your mother's parentage.

We put up at Lord Edward's mother's house in Harley Street in London after the marriage in Tournai. One day a visitor – who had sent a letter prior to her arrival, a letter later read and found comical by Lord Edward's sisters, I must add – was admitted to the house by Tony, while I, who happened to be on the stairs as the door was pulled open, hid behind the tall banister and stared down like a child eavesdropping on its parents. Tony took the visitor straight to the kitchen, for she belonged to a type that could not be shown upstairs. 'I am here to see my daughter Pamela Sims,' said the woman, who had very red hands as I remember, and a shawl tied round her shoulders. 'Please inform her that Mrs Brixey, her mother, is here.'

Well, Pammy, you may consider me a coward when I say that I fled upstairs to the room where Edward sat at the piano and his mother gazed at him from across the room as if she knew him to be a treasure she would soon lose. I had no wish to leave them: my new mamma was Emily, and I silently renounced the woman who had held and fed me by the steaming pans at Christchurch, if this indeed was she. If this Mrs Brixey was your true grandmother, you are from low stock indeed. But you might feel, as I sometimes do, that Mrs Brixey or Mary Sims, woefully lacking in cultivation as she was, made nevertheless a preferable mother to the wicked Madame de Genlis.

The visitor was informed that Lady Edward Fitzgerald was not at home, and was shown from the lower regions of the house – with courtesy, I must say – to the door by the excellent Tony Small. The letter she had sent earlier was discussed for days – for did not the wretched washerwoman announce in no uncertain terms that she was the mother of the young woman just married to the fifth son of the Duchess of Leinster? – and it was finally decided by the Duchess and her son and daughters that the missive and visit both had been some kind of hoax. I was the only one to suspect Madame de Genlis as its perpetrator, if hoax it was, for I knew, from my early years when money was scarce, that a journey to London from the South Coast does not cost nothing; and Tony it was who espied a clutch of *louis d'or* tied in the washerwoman's shawl when she removed it in the kitchen at his invitation and placed it on the back of a chair. This kind of money was seldom seen in England, and Madame de Genlis made a habit of carrying a purse full of *louis* wherever she went. But I kept my suspicions to myself.

None of this, of course, prevented Lord Edward's sisters from arriving at the same conclusion, and I was glad to see they were kind-hearted enough to keep the news of the letter and visit from their mother Emily. 'Surely, our Pam cannot have been a Miss Brixley?' (this is how the name was thought to have been, once the letter and visit had been talked of several times). 'What is Madame de Sillery's game?' And the answer to this I do not know – unless that scheming woman's desire to ensure her reputation remained unblemished lay at the root of all her speeches and actions. I have often thought it would have been kinder to allow me to visit my true mother at the time of our first visit to England, if both Madame de Genlis and the former Mary Sims had wished it.

Little Pam

When I speak to my mother Pamela about Ireland – and again, too, when I press her for more proof of her parentage, as if a memory would suddenly burst from her that would solve the mystery once and for all – she grows animated, then sad. She tells me of the cold corridors of Leinster House where she was immured alone when Lord Edward was under suspicion from the Government, and where she declared she could not creep as far as the nursery for fear of the candles that would be burned and the coal wasted in heating and lighting the great place. 'It was far above what I could afford,' Pamela sighs, and if I wonder at Lord Edward's brother not going so far as to pay for the candles and coal himself I do not say so. For I know my poor mother's mind flits already to the small house in Denzil Street where she hid when her presence at Leinster House meant that Lord Edward would be found and arrested immediately if he came to visit his family.

As for the coal and candles, Pamela cares as little now as she ever did for the vexing subject of money. It was said in Paris that her neglect of the most simple economy was a sign that her father must indeed have been the bankrupted Prince, Philippe of Orléans; and I daresay she has banished from her mind forever the subject of her own four years penniless in the convent at Malabry. But those years of expiation were more recent – and I wonder, even as my mother extols the generosity of her 'dear Mamma' Lord Edward's mother Emily, that she chooses also to forget that the old duchess cut off the allowance set up to educate me, their Little Pam, after the death of her son at Dublin Castle.

To conclude this sad tale of Pamela's apparently endless run of ill fortune at the hands of her relatives, it was also true that she was not for many years able to claim the small allowance settled on her when young by Philippe Egalité. My mother was generous, even if Madame de Genlis was not, I wanted to say to her; but the smallness of the room and the paucity of her possessions here in the Rue Danube make me hesitate before commenting on the gallantry of her nature.

Pamela lives as much in memory of Ireland now as she does in those days when the Revolution burned just a stone's throw from here, and her trustee, M. Barère, one of the last of the Jacobins who had gathered round Madame de Genlis and the Duc d'Orléans in the old days of the Palais Royal, attempted to inculcate the beautiful child with an understanding of money and its importance in the world. And Barère is still in thrall to Pamela, La Belle Pamela as he fondly remembers her, stooping over her hand when he comes to call here at the modest hotel. Only, these days, he brings not deeds for signature nor arithmetic for my mother's instruction, but instead, as he knows her sweet tooth, *mille feuilles*, those glistening confections of pastry notes and cream and jam as rich as a King's ransom, respectfully offered to the woman the old Revolutionary still sees as an eighteen-year-old, setting off for Tournai to marry the good-looking young man she has just met at the Opera. These days, memories and sugar make up Pamela's happiness. And, as she consumes these treasures of sweetness, Pamela – who is still beautiful but, it must be admitted, fat! – shows the pleasure that she loved and gave before Revolution, insurrection and the rest took it all from her. Did Lord Edward find himself intoxicated by the company of a wife who had no ill will – who even, as if the child was no more than an appetising piece of patisserie, a *petit four*, relinquished her only son Eddy to his grandmother without a murmur?

Was my parents' carefree way of being together responsible for the fact that Edward Fitzgerald, leader of the United Irishmen, and his famously revolutionary wife, Pamela Egalité, were almost the last to know of the French attempt to land at Bantry Bay on Christmas Day 1797 and invade Ireland? I do not know; I dare say I was playing at the end of their bed on that morning and showed in no uncertain terms that I had no wish to be interrupted in my own pleasures. But Julie Small would certainly have been present when news finally arrived of the French fleet lost in mist, and a hurricane driving their ships on to the rocks. Julie was my nurse-maid: she must have suffered when her countrymen failed so utterly in their mission to save Ireland on that day. I mention the French girl. 'Oh yes,' my mother says, and now, with her white hands, as soft and lovely as her face can sometimes seem to be, she pulls at the quilts piled on her bed for she complains frequently, even in warm weather, of feeling cold. 'Julie cared for her own little child with Tony Small, at that time: you remember, Pammy, the good Tony Small, Edward's servant who saved your father's life in America? Little Mauricio was suffering pain with his teeth on that day. So the defeat of General Hoche at Bantry Bay was a good deal less important!'

We laugh. Yet I hear the reserve in my mother's voice when she says Julie's name. She pauses, and then goes on.

'I believe,' Pamela says, 'that Julie Small had no thought at first of betraying the trust your father and I had in her – as a Frenchwoman and, of course, as wife of the man to whom your father owed his survival after the battle at Eutaw Springs, the loyal Tony Small. But I found – too late, alas – that a spy, Samuel Turner, a member of our group who had, along with Higgins and the rest, allowed himself to be bought by the British Government, played on Julie's natural desire to found an independent life for herself and her family in London; and he gave her the money and addresses to enable her to do so. Tony would never be told of the provenance of the handsome sums that his wife received from time to time, though it was Tony, at the very end when I was forced to flee for England, who discovered the bribes and asked that they be pardoned – by me, as he knew better than I did then that Lord Edward's wounds worsened and he was likely not to rise from his prison bed in Dublin Castle. This was one battle where Tony Small could not save his dear friend and master. You may imagine how he felt when Julie's giving of information came to light: the poor Small felt responsible for the arrest and death blow of the man he loved most in the world – as well as the cause, through his wife, of a setback for Ireland that was incalculable in its effect. Yet Samuel Turner was, I shall always maintain, the true criminal in this affair. He played on Julie's forgivable instincts – '

'But she should not have told him where the British could find the insurgents,' I cry, for I see my mother's generosity, like a cloud in which right and wrong are obscured, settle around us once more. I understand that the famous passivity of Pamela comes not from a desire to please, as I had once thought, but from the need not to hurt others; despite Julie Small's confession, she will be neither castigated nor blamed. 'Julie in turn saw something – or thought she saw something – which would put me in her power, and enable her to accept the

money she was offered with a clear conscience,' Pamela
says after a long silence. 'Samuel Turner – you will not
remember him, Pam, for you were still a young child;
we were at Hamburg and I was a widow, much sought
after and courted, I regret to say – '

'What is there to regret, when your beauty was
known by everyone and you had lost your husband in
tragic circumstances?' I say, but brusquely, for this false
modesty of my mother's, as I see it, is a throwback to
the hypocrisies and deceit of the ancien régime, when no
one said what they meant, and each compliment carried
its deadly seasoning of ridicule.

'While your father was still alive and we were in
Dublin,' Pamela replies quietly, 'Samuel Turner, one of
those who, as you say, sought my hand in marriage at
Hamburg where I went after being sent out of Ireland
and then England for my treasonable acts' – and here,
smiling up at me from her bed, I see the mischievous
young girl again, who rode in a scarlet habit in front
of the crowd at the Palais Royal – 'Samuel Turner, at
the time Lord Edward was in hiding and I remained in
Leinster House, paid court to me there and then and I
accepted his advances, for I was half-crazed with loneliness and fear. It was this – a certain evening in the long
room lit with only a few candles, and cold for April
with a meagre ration of coal on the fire – that Julie
Small saw. We kissed, Samuel Turner and I, no more
than that. And I never again permitted myself to be
alone with him, for fear he would take further advan-

tage of a woman whose husband, Leader of the Rebels, had no choice but to go along the streets of Dublin dressed as a shepherd or in a woman's clothes. I never did speak in any intimate way to Samuel Turner again, and he suffered from pique: I considered, once his treachery was exposed, that this was a large part of the reason for his betrayal of your father's plan for the meeting in March – '

'Where fifteen men were arrested, and amongst them Arthur O'Connor,' I put in. For my Aunt Lucy, whom Pamela always loved, would tell me of the uprising, and the street fighting in Dublin, and the terrible stroke of ill fortune which befell her brother Lord Edward when he thought himself safe from British soldiers in Thomas Street.

'Yes,' my mother says, and I see she is tired; the memory of those days brings a renewal of the anguish she suffered then. 'And money,' she goes on, her voice faint by now. 'Samuel Turner was well paid for the information he passed on to the British. Julie was recompensed also, no doubt. But to betray Edward, hero to her husband Tony! I was, I confess, most surprised when it became clear that Julie Small was responsible for divulging the secret of Moore the publican's private address. Even though I guessed this at the time – after all, no one else could have confided the secret to Mr Ogilvie with such despatch – I could not reproach Julie. When I made an attempt to remonstrate with her, she spoke slyly to me, and referred to the

evening I had passed in Leinster House with Mr Turner.
I was powerless; and it would not surprise me to hear
that Julie's friend, the kitchen maid at the feather
merchant Mr Murphy's – it was to his house that the
good Moores sent your father when they learned that
their address was known to the authorities – was herself
informed by Julie Small that her employer harboured
a man for whom a warrant had been put out. A reward
of a thousand pounds was offered for the capture and
arrest of your father. I dream still of that house, further
down Thomas Street from the kind Mr Moore, the
house where poor Edward, lying in bed at Murphy's
with a heavy cold, was sprung on and dealt the fatal
blow. I dream of feathers, piled high, escaping and
floating in the wind all night, flying in through the
window of Mr Murphy's house.

'By the time your father was found at the Murphys','
Pamela says, in a voice which is now hardly more than
a whisper, 'I had given birth to my daughter Lucy on the
April night following Mr Ogilvie's loathsome visit, this
succeeded the following night by one of your father's
last escapes from detection, when he visited me in a long
dress and woman's wig at the little house in Denzil
Street. As I say, by the time on that dreadful day in May
of Lord Edward being stabbed and bound and taken to
Newgate Prison, I had been sent with my children to
England and so would never see him again.'

Y

Here, in the history books, the life of my mother Pamela – or at least any further interest in her life – ends. Daughter, so they said in the days of her youth, of the ignoble Duc d'Orléans and the clever, scheming Comtesse de Genlis, the beautiful child brought to the Palais Royal in 1780 at the age of six serves only one purpose for history, if indeed she deserves a footnote at all: as an example of the frivolity of certain aspects of the French Revolution and, later, of the Insurrection in Ireland. We see a figure who seems just as much an invention of the resourceful Comtesse de Genlis as a character in one of her own novels.

Pamela Sims Egalité Capet Fitzgerald Pitcairn deserves, however, a little more than obscurity following the death of her husband Lord Edward in Dublin Castle on 4th June, 1798. From that day to her own death in November 1831, Pamela, like France, had suffered and triumphed, known extreme hardship and happiness and a new freedom. In producing the testimony of those years, and still in search of the truth of my mother's tie with Madame de Genlis, I uncovered memoirs of Pamela's cousin, Henriette de Sercey, in Hamburg; and accounts from Pamela's sister-in-law, Sophia, and of Pamela's younger daughter Lucy, in England. From these I glean as many accurate facts as I can, for my mother, as autumn sent its darkness into the Rue Danube in the last year of her life, became sleepy and forgetful of the long years since my father's death. She believed, at times, that her mother, as diabolical as the author of *Les Liaisons Dangereuses*, had enjoyed a lengthy liaison with Philippe Duc d'Orléans, and to avoid the consequences had always insisted the two little adopted girls were no more than that. At other times, she called herself Pamela Sims or Brixey and said that Nathaniel Forth, sent to England to find a pretty little girl and a fine mare, had done just that. He was not guided by the Duc d'Orléans and Madame de Genlis towards a secret child of their own; and Pamela would say laughing that the continual assertions on the part of Madame de Genlis that she was not the mother of Pamela may well have constituted one of the rare occasions on which she actually told the truth.

γ

Pamela sleeps, and as I tell the autobiography of my mother, I close my eyes so we are both, in the brown light of a winter afternoon in Paris, dreaming the same story – the difference between us being that I must imagine as far back as I can to a November day thirty-three years ago, and Pamela need only remember.

We are in Hamburg and we have come to stay with Henriette. I am four years old. Pamela is here, but her likeness has preceded her. Wherever I go, I see the image of the widow, a black veil over her head. She is seated, and I am kneeling, face buried in my mother's dress. My brother is in her arms. This is the heroine of the moment, this saint who dispenses kindness to all, but has received nothing but harshness from the cruel British who have murdered her husband, the Rebel leader Lord Edward Fitzgerald. No matter that the ages of the children are quite wrong in this picture; and no matter, either, that it does not appear possible for the artist to have been George Romney, as is said – this portrayal of afflicted beauty is the most purchased and talked-about item in all of Hamburg. Even Mr Matthieson, who likes to finish his breakfast early and start on his figures in the study, stays staring down at the sad face of La Belle Pamela. I could swear he is as much in love with her by now as those who come enquiring if Lady Edward is ready yet to receive them. Colonel Harcourt is one of these and, amongst all the others, I am most smiled and winked at by a Mr Turner, who has a most impertinent manner, and Mr Pitcairn, an American. How am I to keep all these importunate suitors from the door, while my mother weeps upstairs and Julie hustles her own child Mauricio out at the back, so the daughter of the hero Lord Edward Fitzgerald can play undisturbed? Even if I can't understand what is happening here, I scent the prurient interest and sheer excitement of the would-be husbands and the newspaper reporters who write poignant accounts of Pamela's loneliness and misery, and, if not that, salacious tales of her lovemaking with a host of exiled Irishmen.

Which star was 'la pauvre Pamela' born under, that the most flamboyant and dastardly actions take place wherever she goes? I heard my aunt Lady Henry Fitzgerald say yesterday that her sister-in-law Lady Henry says that she fears that Lady Edward will stir up revolutionary fervour in the breasts of all she meets, and that Lord Henry, who wrote a very fierce letter to the Viceroy of Ireland following the death in Dublin Castle of his brother, has been prevented from thinking of coming out here to visit the sad widow. Pamela is considered dangerous by so many, yet there was never a mother gentler or sweeter – even if she does, at times, complain too much. For she has a good friend here in Henriette, and many friends who pay her the most respectful compliments, and above all she has me to cheer her and make her laugh when she is sad.

Besides this, I can tell that one or two of the suitors appear to please Pamela, when she is in the mood to bear their siege of our house and their requests to see her. There will be a dinner tonight, at which Mr Pitcairn will be present. He is the best of them, I believe; and I sense also that my mother will one day think so too. I know, if she does marry this American, it will be for my protection and not for love. No one will ever replace my father in my mother's heart.

Pamela speaks sometimes of my father's mother, the 'Dear Mamma' to whom she gave her treasure, little Eddy, anew after the tragic death of our father. She had turned to the Duchess as to a true mother, so she often told me as she wept and I comforted her – and when Madame de Genlis, in a letter I carried up to her, asked that Pamela and myself, her Little Pam, come to live with her, the offer was refused. Now, Pamela says she has no mother at all. I wish all the people who stare in the windows and Mr Turner and Mr Pitcairn and all the gentlemen who want to take me on their knee would go away, and we could be left to live in peace.

𝒴

It is November, and Pamela lies dying in the Hotel Danube. Dawn breaks and I see she can no longer tell if the twilight belongs to evening or to day. She asks if All Saints is today when a flower-seller in the street below calls out her wares: chrysanthemums or a posy of violets for those who still may walk and go dancing under the last leaves of the trees, or a sprig of yew, which brings tears to my mother's eyes when I bring it in for her, a memento of the dinner at Belle-Chasse thirty-three years ago where she and my father met and fell in love.

As she wakes and sleeps, dreams and memories come to Pamela, and I write them as she speaks. The years of expiation of the debts my poor mother incurred both in England and France are as close to her still as the grim walls of the convent at Malabry where she was immured for four years at the behest of Madame de Genlis. I see the cloistered walks, the downward gaze of the nuns as they pass the woman who is punished for her lack of knowledge of the worth of money, and who received nothing from the famous Gouverneur of the

Orléans children. Madame de Genlis, my mother says, is on the best of terms with the Emperor Napoleon. He has awarded her a pension and a fine set of rooms. But 'Maman', whom everyone supposes to be the mother of Pamela, has made no provision for her daughter. 'She even wanted me to leave Paris, for fear of compromising her standing with the Buonapartes,' my mother goes on, and she laughs, pulling herself up in bed and catching her own reflection in the windows that open out on to a meagre balcony above the cries of traders and the crowd. I see she is flushed, and I know she finds a reason for a last show of triumph before she falls back exhausted on to the pillows I have piled high behind her. 'When I pleaded with Madame de Genlis to be allowed to stay in the city – to avoid the horrors of the convent at Malabry – she told me not to go around boasting that I was her daughter. "For, Pamela, you are not." Those, Little Pam, were her words.'

'And your reply, mamma?' I say quietly, for I have listened to this story of my mother's repartee many times before.

'Why, Little Pam, I simply retorted that if I were, it would be nothing to boast about,' says my mother. And we smile in unison – as if, I cannot help but reflect, my poor mother's one occasion of rudeness to the woman who reared her as her own could make much difference to anything in the end.

The light strengthens and Pamela pulls her hand-mirror up to her face, so I pass her, as I invariably do, the rouge and creams she needs – to face a visit from the old Duc de Force, most likely, or on occasion an ancient Revolutionary from the days of Egalité, limbs creaking as he bows over the bed.

But my mother stares out of the window now, at the sound of horses' hooves in the narrow cobbled street that is the Rue Danube. 'You know, in the end, Julie felt guilt at betraying Edward's whereabouts,' my mother whispers, as exhausted now as if she had travelled to Ireland and had just arrived at break of day in the house in Denzil Street where her true life and her marriage ended. 'Julie went to Mr Murphy's on that night when poor Edward was stabbed and taken.' With a hand that is not swollen like the rest of her – fingers as slender and pale as the young harp-player's in the picture – Pamela brushes the jars of cream and eye-shadow to the floor and, as she speaks, her voice grows low and her breath is uneven. 'Julie told young Molly at Mr Murphy's to batter the beefsteaks until they are thin,' and here Pamela smiles, 'as I had taught her to, in Paris when we were there together. Then she should leave them an hour or so and cover with pepper quickly. Edward would think of me when he ate them and the strength from the meal would help him evade his pursuers.'

I hang my head, and for the first time feel pity for Julie Small who so much regretted her betrayal of my father. I had not heard of the beefsteaks – and, like my mother's, my eyes fill with tears. For we both know too well the ending of that night at the feather-merchant's house: how Lord Edward had called out at hearing foot-steps on the stairs, that Murphy had replied that it was 'only the beefsteaks'; and that Molly, in panic, dropped the dish and ran straight to Dublin Castle. My father had no chance of escape from that time on. 'And Julie writes that Molly got no more than a few banknotes for her trouble,' Pamela finishes. But she can no longer smile.

For the rest of my mother's story, I add here an extract from the Journal of Henriette de Sercey (Mrs Matthie-son), written on 23 July 1800, in Hamburg. I was too young at that time to understand the marriage of Pamela, or its eventual disastrous ending; and certainly could not fathom the deep currents of feeling between Madame de Genlis and my mother. Who Pamela really was – and who I may be – will remain a mystery. But at the time of my mother's marriage to the American, she was considered to be the daughter of Madame de Genlis and Philippe Egalité. That she was publicly shown to be no such thing must have been hard for her to bear.

Journal of Henriette de Sercey

Yesterday my very dear friend Pamela, Lady Edward Fitzgerald, married Mr Joseph Pitcairn in the Spanish Chapel. I wish them all the happiness in the world; and I pray that my poor friend will know peace at last, after a life of storms: at twenty-seven years old, and with the need still, as she has proclaimed, to 'love and be loved,' I can only give expression to my hope that the right choice has been made between the suitors. Mr Turner, I am told, had gone off to England in pique, where he was immediately arrested and is held at Fort George; the others, wearing an air of dejection, have melted away. I have warned Pamela, in the days preceding the wedding (postponed while waiting for the arrival in Hamburg of Madame de Genlis), that she must be certain she marries 'for love and the need to be loved', and that it is never too late to annul the ceremony and wait until true love finally appears. I know well that the poor soul is of the opinion that no one can ever replace Lord Edward, in her affections or in the world altogether, so great was his courage and so numerous his qualities – but I fear the marriage with Mr Pitcairn takes place for the reason that it is better to have an *état*, as the French have it, than to have none at all: in short, it is better by far to be married than single or a widow. I believe Pamela makes a mistake in giving her consent to the American consul – an upright Protestant who will not let her go hungry or ignored, but I do not believe she loves him. She seems happy enough, though; I can only trust that she will cleave to him as she did to her adored husband.

It is easy to see why the beautiful but bewildered Pamela should find herself in need of some assurances of who and what she may be in the world. Her mother, my aunt Madame de Genlis, who came to Hamburg two days ago, produced a thunderbolt in this very house on the evening before the wedding; and I must confess surprise that my poor angel Pamela was able to go ahead with the nuptial rites at the chapel the following day – or that Mr Pitcairn, who must be unused to the kind of melodramatic tale his about-to-be mother-in-law produced, felt ready and able to become Pamela's spouse. I imagine Tante Félicité simply lost the will to give what had practically been promised as an announcement of the true origins of Pamela on the eve of the dear girl's second marriage – and said the opposite instead. We were all thrown into confusion; and Mr Matthieson proclaimed later that he had no desire to see more of my aunt if she intended to continue in this paradoxical way. This is what took place, in my salon, with a good number of friends assembled to hear Pamela's mother – as all of course accepted her to be – give a gracious address in honour of Lady Edward and Mr Pitcairn.

The first thing I noticed – and have seldom witnessed in all the years I have known my aunt – was the extreme agitation of Madame de Genlis on this occasion. She had, it was true, taken communion and confession before our gathering; it was an extremely hot evening; and at first I assumed, as I know others did also, that the emotion engendered by a public announcement of her true relationship with Pamela (for this had never taken place before) must be responsible for the pallor and downcast regard with which she confronted us. The room grew silent – the children were stopped from chattering in the background – and, without preamble, the great educationalist and author solemnly assured the assembled wedding guests that Pamela was the daughter of a humble English washerwoman, and had been bought for hard cash! You may imagine the shocked whispers which ran around my salon at this quite unexpected declaration . . . Poor Pamela fainted and Mr Pitcairn looked most uneasy. Only Mr Matthieson had the presence of mind to fetch water and assist the couple on the eve of their wedding day.

I continue here eighteen years after the event I have found briefly described in my Journal; and I wonder, as so often is the case in life, at the discrepancy between the hopes and prayers so fervently offered for happiness and mutual love between dear friends and the reality – in this case a misunderstanding so deep and beyond repair that there can be no hope for recovery.

I welcomed Pamela this week to the Château de Carlepont, near Noyon, where I am happily installed with my husband M. de Finguerlin (for whom I left Mr Matthieson and was divorced by him: I have no regrets on that score). She and I embraced delightedly, as we always do; and the sad further happenings in that poor martyr's life are not referred to, nor will they be, for the duration of her stay here. I wish only for Pamela to remember the fine things of her past experience: her true love with the hero Edward Fitzgerald; her adoration of her daughter, Little Pam, taken, alas!, from her mother, just as little Eddy and the child Lucy had been, and handed over to the Fitzgerald family to rear; and the strength of her loyalty to Madame de Genlis, my aunt, who brought up Pamela as her daughter and then in the end renounced her.

As for Mr Pitcairn, I fear it was a revulsion to the debts his wife ran up that made it so practicable for that good American to pretend he believed all the gossip and vile slander put about on the subject of my angelic friend Pamela. I know, after a visit from Hamburg to England at least ten years ago, that poor Pamela found it necessary to borrow from young Casimir, a musician adopted by Madame de Genlis, in order to gain a passage in a packet boat going from Dover to Calais.

The boat belonged to Count Esterhazy; and Little Pam – for she was still under the supervision of her mother – was requested to dress up as a boy in order to travel on a fake passport. Pamela was trying, in her flight to France, to escape her creditors in London and to receive in Paris the allowance settled on her by the Duc d'Orléans all those years ago. But Mr Pitcairn chose to believe the wicked whispers, which said that Pamela Pitcairn had eloped with Count Esterhazy; he took their daughter Helen permanently into his care, and my sad friend soon found herself alone and equally pursued by creditors in the Paris of Napoleon Buonaparte. To my eternal shame, I must admit that my aunt, on finding her daughter in need and requesting assistance from her, wrote to the Emperor denouncing this young woman 'to whom I owe nothing, and who owes me everything'. I prefer not to dwell on the four years of penance suffered by Pamela at the convent of Malabry, as she worked off her debts; and I applaud my friend settling at Abbaye-Aux-Bois, where she has Madame de Récamier as a companion – though it is hard to imagine these two beauties, so unalike in temperament, finding pleasure in each other's company.'

Little Pam

*H*ere the journal of Henriette de Finguerlin breaks off. I, Pamela Campbell, staying at my mother's bedside until the end, report that Pamela Sims Egalité, as she had once been known, died peacefully this morning, 7th November 1831, and that she spoke of two dreams, as she drifted in and out of consciousness, these recurring so frequently that she was persuaded of their not being dreams at all, but reality.

The first, as I have described to my own daughters, was of a meadow with tall grass and wild flowers, situated on a river bank; and of a woman, very pretty, with chocolate eyes and loose hair, who ran up from the river in a dress that billowed out behind her. It was a fine day in spring. The other, which took place in a dark, snowbound landscape on the edge of a great sea of ice, was harder to understand, but the more persistent of the two; and this I have tried to imagine as I heard it at the Hotel Danube in the last hours of the mysterious woman known in her youth as La Belle Pamela.

Also available from
THE MAIA PRESS

PEMBERLEY REVISITED
Emma Tennant

The best-selling sequels to *Pride and Prejudice* now reprinted in one volume

'It is a truth universally acknowledged, that a married man in possession of a good fortune must be in want of a son and heir'

Elizabeth wins Darcy, and Jane wins Bingham – but do they 'live happily ever after'? Emma Tennant's sequels to *Pride and Prejudice* ingeniously pick up several threads from Jane Austen's timeless novel, in a lighthearted and affectionate look at the possible subsequent lives of all the main characters. *Pemberley* tells of Elizabeth's failure to produce a child; while *An Unequal Marriage* continues the story of the Bennets and their circle into the next generation. Sparkling, stylish and ironic, with imaginative insights into the emotions and mores of eighteenth-century English high society, these are elegant and diverting social comedies by a master of the genre.

'Emma Tennant's narrative is made compelling by her utter mastery of Austen's style'—*The New York Times Books Review*
'A treat for Janeites, written with great comic finesse'—*Mail on Sunday*

£8.99 ISBN 1 904559 17 4

WILD DOGS
Helen Humphreys

Out beyond the edge of town, in the woods behind Cooper's farm, a pack of lost dogs run wild. At dusk every evening six people gather to call their former companions home. Their patient waiting becomes a ritual, a memorial and then a healing, as they share their common losses and individual stories. In her fourth novel, Helen Humphreys weaves an enchanting tapestry of characters, layering lyrical narrative and rich imagery into a work of deep resonance and delicate hope. Beginning with the simple and evocative image of dogs that have chosen the wild, each scene draws the reader further towards a compelling reminder of our instinctive need to connect and be a part of a larger whole. *Wild Dogs* is a remarkable work about the power of human strength, trust and love.

'A compelling story of loss and of truth, simply and beautifully rendered: *Wild Dogs* is a gem'—Gillian Slovo

£8.99 ISBN 1 904559 15 8

UNITY Michael Arditti

'Strikingly original
... a remarkable,
unsettling book'—
The Times
'The most intriguing
and thought-
provoking novel I
have read this year'
—*Daily Express*
£8.99
ISBN 1 904559 12 3

Michael Arditti's fourth novel examines the
personalities and politics involved in the making of a
film about the relationship between Unity Mitford and
Hitler, set against the background of the Red Army
Faction terror campaign in 1970s Germany. Almost
thirty years after the film was abandoned following its
leading actress's participation in a terrorist attack, the
narrator sets out to uncover her true motives. In this
deeply disturbing picture of corruption and fanaticism
in Britain and Germany from the 1930s to today,
Arditti presents a profound, and timely, exploration
of the nature of evil.

THE GLORIOUS FLIGHT OF PERDITA TREE

Olivia Fane

'Smart, fluid prose
and sophisticated
thought ... a
thoughtful,
sorrowful and
highly amusing
novel'—*The Times*
£8.99
ISBN 1 904559 13 1

Perdita Tree, the bored and beautiful wife of a Tory
MP, believes that all women should have a magic door
through which they can walk into a different life. So
when she is kidnapped in Albania, she takes it in the
spirit of a huge adventure. Adored by her kidnapper,
who believes all things English are perfect, she is
persuaded to rescue the Albanians from their dire
history, and is vain enough to imagine that she can.
The year is 1991, democracy is coming, but are the
Albanians ready for it? And are they ready for Perdita?

UNDERWORDS: THE HIDDEN CITY

The Booktrust London Short Story Competition Anthology

'A feast of spicy
dialogue and
compelling
narrative ...
a *must-buy*'—
Mslexia
£9.99
ISBN 1 904559 14 X

London has always revealed itself in a multitude of
different guises, each as individual as the dreams and
aspirations of its many inhabitants. The theme of this
collection is the hidden city, with fourteen stories
vividly expressing different moods and aspects of the
capital, and its irrepressible mixture of excitement or
tension, fear or freedom. Featuring six new stories
plus work by **Diran Adebayo**, **Nicola Barker**,
Romesh Gunesekera, **Sarah Hall**, **Hanif Kureishi**,
Andrea Levy, **Patrick Neate** and **Alex Wheatle**.

OCEANS OF TIME Merete Morken Andersen

'Artistry and intensity of vision'—*Guardian*
'An intensely moving novel'—*Independent*
'A bravely clear-eyed study'—*The Times*
£8.99
ISBN 1 904559 11 5

A long-divorced couple face a family tragedy in the white night of a Norwegian summer. Forced to confront what went wrong in their relationship, they plumb the depths of sorrow and despair before emerging with a new understanding. This profound novel deals with loss and grief, but also, transformingly, with hope, recovery and love.
Translated from Norwegian by Barbara J. Haveland
Chosen as an International Book of the Year, TLS
LONGLISTED FOR INDEPENDENT FOREIGN FICTION PRIZE 2005
SHORTLISTED FOR OXFORD WEIDENFELD TRANSLATION PRIZE 2005. NOMINATED FOR THE IMPAC AWARD 2006

ESSENTIAL KIT Linda Leatherbarrow

'Full of acute observation, surprising imagery and even shocks … joyously surreal … gnomically funny, and touching'—Shena Mackay
£8.99
ISBN 1 904559 10 7

In these varied and exquisite short stories, Linda Leatherbarrow brings together for the first time her prize-winning short prose with new and previously unpublished work. A wide-ranging, rich and surprising gallery of characters includes a nineteen-year-old girl leaving home, a talking gorilla in the swinging sixties, a shoe fetishist and a long-distance walker. The prose is lyrical, witty and uplifting, funny and moving, always pertinent – proving that the short story is the perfect literary form for contemporary urban life.

RUNNING HOT Dreda Say Mitchell

'An exciting new voice in urban fiction'—*Guardian*
'Sharp-eyed, even sharper-tongued chase story'—*Literary Review*
'Swaggeringly cool and incredibly funny'—*Stirling Observer*
£8.99
ISBN 1 904559 09 3

Elijah 'Schoolboy' Campbell is heading out of London's underworld, a world where bling, ringtones and petty deaths are accessories of life. He's taking a great offer to leave it all behind and start a new life, but the problem is he's got no spare cash. He stumbles across a mobile phone, but it is marked property, and the Street won't care that he found it by accident. The door to redemption is only open for seven days. Schoolboy knows that when you're running hot, all it takes is one call or one message to disconnect you from this life – permanently. Mitchell was born into London's Grenadian community. This is her first novel.

GOOD CLEAN FUN Michael Arditti

'Witheringly funny, painfully acute'— *Literary Review*
'Assured in tone ... this moving work rings true'— *Independent*
£8.99
ISBN 1 904559 08 5

This dazzling first collection of short stories from an award-winning author employs a host of remarkable characters and a range of original voices to take an uncompromising look at love and loss in the twenty-first century. These twelve stories of contentment and confusion, defiance and desire, are marked by wit, compassion and insight. Michael Arditti was born in Cheshire and lives in London. He is the author of four highly acclaimed novels, *The Celibate*, *Pagan and her Parents*, *Easter* and *Unity*.

A BLADE OF GRASS Lewis DeSoto

'A plangent debut ... an extremely persuasive bit of storytelling' —*Daily Mail*
'Outstanding debut novel' —*The Times*
£8.99
ISBN 1 904559 07 7

Märit Laurens farms with her husband near the border of South Africa. When guerrilla violence and tragedy visit their lives, Märit finds herself in a tug of war between the local Afrikaaners and the black farmworkers. Lyrical and profound, this exciting novel offers a unique perspective on what it means to be black and white in a country where both live and feel entitlement. DeSoto, born in South Africa, emigrated to Canada in the 1960s. This is his first novel.
LONGLISTED FOR THE MAN BOOKER PRIZE 2004
SHORTLISTED FOR THE ONDAATJE PRIZE 2005

PEPSI AND MARIA Adam Zameenzad

'A beautifully crafted, multi-faceted book: a highly dramatic and gripping thriller and a searing indictment of cruelty and inhumanity'—*New Internationalist*
£8.99
ISBN 1 904559 06 9

Pepsi is a smart street kid in an unnamed South American country. His mother is dead and his father, a famous politician, has disowned him. He rescues the kidnapped Maria, but they must both escape the sadistic policeman Caddy whose obsession is to kill them – as personal vendetta and also as part of his crusade to rid the city of the 'filth' of street children. In this penetrating insight into the lives of the dispossessed, the author conveys the children's exhilarating zest for life and beauty, which triumphs over the appalling reality of their lives. Adam Zameenzad was born in Pakistan and lives in London. His previous novels have been published to great acclaim in many languages. This is his sixth novel.

UNCUT DIAMONDS
edited by Maggie Hamand

'The ability to pin down a moment or a mindset breathes from these stories … They're all stunning, full of wonderful characters'—
Big Issue
£7.99
ISBN 1 904559 03 4

Vibrant, original stories showcasing the huge diversity of new writing talent in contemporary London. They include an incident in a women's prison; a spiritual experience in a motorway service station; a memory of growing up in sixties Britain and a lyrical West Indian love story. Unusual and sometimes challenging, this collection gives voice to previously unpublished writers from a wide diversity of backgrounds whose experiences – critical to an understanding of contemporary life in the UK – often remain hidden from view.

ANOTHER COUNTRY   Hélène du Coudray

'The descriptions of the refugee Russians are agonisingly lifelike' —review of 1st edition, *Times Literary Supplement*
£7.99
ISBN 1 904559 04 2

Ship's officer Charles Wilson arrives in Malta in the early 1920s, leaving his wife and children behind in London. He falls for a Russian émigrée governess, the beautiful Maria Ivanovna, and the passionate intensity of his feelings propels him into a course of action that promises to end in disaster. This prize-winning novel, first published in 1928, was written by an Oxford undergraduate, Hélène Héroys, who was born in Kiev in 1906. She went on to write a biography of Metternich, and three further novels.

THE THOUSAND-PETALLED DAISY
Norman Thomas

'This novel, both rhapsody and lament, is superb'—
Independent on Sunday
£7.99
ISBN 1 904559 05 0

Injured in a riot while travelling in India, 17-year-old Michael Flower is given shelter in a white house on an island. There, accompanied by his alter ego (his glove-puppet Mickey-Mack), he meets Om Prakash and his family, a tribe of holy monkeys, the beautiful Lila and a mysterious holy woman. Jealousy and violence, a death and a funeral, the delights of first love and the beauty of the landscape are woven into a narrative infused with a distinctive, offbeat humour. Norman Thomas was born in Wales in 1926. His first novel was published in 1963. He lives in Auroville, South India.

ON BECOMING A FAIRY GODMOTHER
Sara Maitland

'Funny, surreal tales
. . . magic and
mystery'—*Guardian*
'These tales
insistently fill the
vison'—*Times
Literary Supplement*
£7.99
ISBN 1 904559 00 X

Fifteen 'fairy stories' breathe new life into old legends and bring the magic of myth back into modern women's lives. What became of Helen of Troy, of Guinevere and Maid Marion? And what happens to today's mature woman when her children have fled the nest? Here is an encounter with a mermaid, an erotic adventure with a mysterious stranger, the story of a woman who learns to fly and another who transforms herself into a fairy godmother.

IN DENIAL Anne Redmon

'A discomforting
yet compelling
work. Graceful and
gratifyingly rigorous'
— *Mslexia*
'Intricate, thoughtful'
—*TLS*
£7.99
ISBN 1 904559 01 8

In a London prison a serial offender, Gerry Hythe, is gloating over the death of his one-time prison visitor Harriet Washington. He thinks he is in prison once again because of her. Anne Redmon weaves evidence from the past and present of Gerry's life into a chilling mystery. A novel of great intelligence and subtlety, *In Denial* explores themes which are usually written about in black and white, but here are dealt with in all their true complexity.

LEAVING IMPRINTS Henrietta Seredy

'This mesmerising,
poignant novel
creates an intense
atmosphere'—
Publishing News
'Compelling ... full
of powerful events
and emotions'—
Oxford Times
£7.99
ISBN 1 904559 02 6

'At night when I can't sleep I imagine myself on the island.' But Jessica is alone in a flat by a park. She doesn't want to be there – she doesn't have anywhere else to go. As the story moves between present and past, gradually Jessica reveals the truth behind the compelling relationship that has dominated her life. 'With restrained lyricism, *Leaving Imprints* explores a destructive, passionate relationship between two damaged people. Its quiet intensity does indeed leave imprints. I shall not forget this novel'—Sue Gee, author of *The Hours of the Night*